"You worry too much about things 'ruining your life....'"

Willow knew her grandmother was referring to more than her amnesia-related recognition problem. She'd always thought Willow had overdramatized the humiliating incident that had turned her parents against her and changed the course of her life, that she'd been too quick to thrust all the blame on Cal Chandler. Okay, so it wasn't *all* his fault. No one had forced her to sleep with Cal. She'd just loved him so fiercely, and she'd been so afraid of losing him. How could she know her parents would catch them?

"I wish he'd just get married," she mumbled. Then maybe she could *really* forget him and move on.

"He still pines for you, you know. You can't hate a man forever simply because he loved you too much."

Willow chuckled. "He didn't love me. He was horny and ruined my life."

"You know he loved you," Nana scolded. "And still does…"

Dear Reader,

Imagine being unable to recognize your own mother—or your ex-lover. This is the dilemma Willow Marsden faces in *The Forgotten Cowboy*. (If you read *The Millionaire Next Door*, my previous Harlequin American Romance novel, you might remember that Willow was injured in a car accident during a tornado.)

Willow's condition is known as prosopagnosia, and it really does exist. I became aware of it when reading a book about how to improve your memory. I was fascinated, and the first thing I thought of (predictably) was *What if I created a character with this disorder? And what if she couldn't recognize her ex-boyfriend, with whom she shared a disastrous past?* It's always fun to come up with a new way to cause trouble for my characters.

If you would like to learn more about this unusual disorder and hear firsthand from people who cope with it every day, check out the Internet for extensive information.

I love to hear from readers!
E-mail me at karalennox@yahoo.com
or contact me via regular mail at P.O. Box 4845,
Dallas, TX 75148.

All best,

Kara Lennox

THE FORGOTTEN COWBOY
Kara Lennox

TORONTO • NEW YORK • LONDON
AMSTERDAM • PARIS • SYDNEY • HAMBURG
STOCKHOLM • ATHENS • TOKYO • MILAN • MADRID
PRAGUE • WARSAW • BUDAPEST • AUCKLAND

ISBN 0-373-75056-0

THE FORGOTTEN COWBOY

Copyright © 2005 by Kara Lennox.

Books by Kara Lennox

HARLEQUIN AMERICAN ROMANCE

841—VIRGIN PROMISE
856—TWIN EXPECTATIONS
871—TAME AN OLDER MAN
893—BABY BY THE BOOK
917—THE UNLAWFULLY WEDDED PRINCESS
934—VIXEN IN DISGUISE*
942—PLAIN JANE'S PLAN*
951—SASSY CINDERELLA*
974—FORTUNE'S TWINS
990—THE MILLIONAIRE NEXT DOOR
1052—THE FORGOTTEN COWBOY

*How To Marry a Hardison

Don't miss any of our special offers. Write to us at the
following address for information on our newest releases.

Harlequin Reader Service
U.S.: 3010 Walden Ave., P.O. Box 1325, Buffalo, NY 14269
Canadian: P.O. Box 609, Fort Erie, Ont. L2A 5X3

Prologue

Willow Marsden studied the strange woman in her hospital room. She was an attractive female in her twenties, her beauty marred by a black eye and a bandage wound around her head. The woman looked unfamiliar; she was a complete stranger. Unfortunately, the stranger was in Willow's mirror.

She lay the mirror down with a long sigh. *Prosopagnosia*—that was the clinical name for her condition. She'd suffered a head injury during a car accident, which had damaged a very specific portion of her brain—the part that enabled humans to distinguish one face from another. For Willow, every face she saw was strange and new to her—even those of her closest friends and relatives.

"You're telling me I could be like this forever?"

Dr. Patel, her neurologist, shrugged helplessly. "Every recovery is different. You could snap back to normal in a matter of days, weeks, months or…yes, the damage could be permanent."

"What about my short-term memory?" She couldn't even remember what she'd had for breakfast that morning.

Again a shrug. Why was it so difficult to get a straight answer out of a doctor?

"Do you think I'll be up to speed for medical school in the fall?" She asked the question as casually as she dared.

Dr. Patel abruptly dropped his professional-doctor mask. "I didn't know of your plans. I'm sorry."

"I guess that's a big, fat no." Willow softened her comment with a smile, but she had to force it. She should be grateful to be alive, to be walking and talking with no disfiguring scars. Her car accident during last week's tornado had been a serious one and she easily could have died if not for the speed and skill of her rescuers. Right now, though, she didn't feel grateful at all. Her plans and dreams were in serious jeopardy.

Dr. Patel closed Willow's chart and offered a tentative smile. "Sometimes life throws us curve balls. But if your dream is to be a healer, you will find a way."

Maybe, but not at University of Texas Southwestern. Willow had fought so hard to be accepted in the first place. If she withdrew at this late date with no explanation, she had very little chance of being accepted again. And if she told them the truth…well, no medical school wants a student with cognitive dysfunction.

For Willow, that meant only one thing. She would recover sooner rather than later. Damn the prognosis. She was not going to let anyone—not even fate—snatch away her dreams.

Not this time.

She was in control of her future. In six weeks, she intended to be at med school with a fully functioning brain.

Chapter One

One week later, Willow pasted on a smile as yet another wedding guest approached the register book. This was much, much harder than she'd anticipated.

"Why, Willow, it's so good to see you up and around!" The woman was in her fifties, fashionably dressed, slender. The man with her was balding, wore glasses, carried himself with an air of self-importance.

Now, who in Cottonwood fit that description? Only about a zillion people. "I'm feeling much better," Willow responded, plucking the white-plumed pen from its stand and holding it out. The woman took the hint and signed the book. Willow read the signature upside-down, a skill she was quickly acquiring. *The Honorable and Mrs. Milton Chatsworth*. Duh! The mayor and his wife. Their daughter, Anne, had been Willow's favorite babysitter.

"How's your granddaughter doing?" Willow asked. Anne was now married and the mother of a darling baby daughter.

"Growing like a weed," the mayor crowed. "Do you want to see pictures?" He reached for his wallet, but his wife, Deborah, stopped him.

"Now, Milton, Willow's busy. Maybe she can look at the pictures later." She gave Willow a shoulder-squeeze and the couple moved on.

Willow breathed a sigh of relief as she surreptitiously jotted notes on an index card under the table skirt. *Deb. Chatsworth. Teal dress, emerald ring.* She'd given up on cataloguing the men. They were *all* wearing gray suits and navy ties. It was as if they'd called each other last night and arranged to match. But if she could keep the women straight, that might work, since couples tended to stick together. Unfortunately, she had to write down the cues, since her memory was still so spasmodic.

At first, she hadn't wanted to attend her friend Mick's wedding. It had sounded like her worst nightmare—a hundred people she knew, all of them with the same face. Then she'd reasoned that if she was going to cure her brain problem, she had to put herself in challenging situations and exercise her gray cells. And so far, so good. No one had even suspected she had a problem.

She turned her attention to the couple approaching her table. Ugh, another man in a gray suit. This one had blond hair and was undoubtedly handsome, though she could only judge that by objectively cataloguing his regular features, blue eyes and square jaw.

Her heart skipped a beat. Oh, please, don't let it be him. Don't let it be Cal Chandler. She was in no mood to face him, not when he was with a shapely woman in a snug red dress. Though it was tempting to rub his face in the fact that she was off to medical school in five weeks, despite everything he'd done to wreck her life, she wouldn't be able to gloat with any sincerity—not when her future was again in doubt.

Just thinking about him started a slow burn in her gut. She'd gotten her life back on track despite the devastating setback she'd suffered five years ago, but she couldn't say the same about him. He was practically a genius, with a degree in biomedical science. But he'd blown off vet school after one year and was now wasting his life as a casual laborer on a ranch. Not that it wasn't good, honest work, but with Cal's potential—

"Willow," the woman in the red dress said with a warm smile as she signed the book. "I didn't expect to see you here. You look a little flushed—are you okay?"

Willow glanced at the signature and sighed with quiet relief. This handsome blond man was Jeff Hardison, her grandmother's doctor, and his wife, Allison, Cottonwood's dentist. She was spared Cal for the moment.

Willow summoned a smile. "I'm feeling great."

"Are you sure? I could bring you some punch."

"Oh, no, I'm fine," Willow said reassuringly. "It's just a little warm in here." Or maybe it was just her. It burned her up just thinking about all the opportunities Cal had tossed away while she'd toiled through college working three jobs—

Okay, she had to stop thinking about him or she was going to embarrass herself.

"It's good to see you," Jeff said, sincerity tingeing his voice. "You had the whole town worried for a few days."

"I appreciate the concern, but I'm fine now."

As the Hardisons walked away, Willow realized her grandmother was standing beside her. Pathetically, she only knew it was Nana because she recognized her gaudy rhinestone brooch.

"Any problems?" her grandmother asked in a stage whisper. "You know, recognizing people?"

"I've got a pretty good system going." Willow showed Nana her stack of index cards with their hastily written hints. "No one suspects a thing."

"I don't know why you don't want anyone to know," Nana said. "It's nothing to be embarrassed about."

"Nana, think about it. Do you want the whole town to think I'm brain-damaged? Even once I make a full recovery, that's a label that could stick with me and ruin my life."

Nana clucked like a fussy hen. "You worry too much about things 'ruining your life.'"

Willow knew her grandmother was referring to more than the recent accident. She'd always thought Willow had overdramatized the humiliating incident that had turned her parents against her and changed the course of her life, that she'd been too quick to thrust all the blame on Cal. Okay, so it wasn't *all* his fault. No one had held a gun to her head and forced her to take her clothes off and have sex with Cal. But she'd loved Cal so fiercely, and had been so afraid of losing him, she might as well have had a gun to her head when he'd taken her virginity.

"He's here, you know," Nana said quietly.

Willow didn't have to clarify to whom Nana was referring. Her blood pressure ratcheted up a knot. "He is? Where is he? What's he wearing? Wait, let me guess. A gray suit?"

"Why, yes. How did you know that?"

Willow smiled despite herself. "Statistical analysis. Nana, how will I know him so I can avoid him?"

"Don't worry. I think he's avoiding you. He didn't sign the guest book, after all. But just in case, he's wearing a red carnation in his lapel."

"All right. That should be easy enough to spot. Um, Nana, is he here with anyone?"

"You mean, a date?"

Willow nodded, shame washing through her that she even cared. She shouldn't.

"I didn't notice any particular girls with him."

"I wish he'd just get married," Willow mumbled. Then maybe she could *really* forget him and move on.

"He still pines after you, you know."

Willow thrust out her jaw. "Let him pine." As if he really would. He probably had a line of women following him around.

"To err is human," Nana said. "To forgive, divine."

Willow had no snappy comeback for that one. "I know I should forgive him," she said softly. "It's wrong to carry a grudge. Sometimes I pray that I'll find the grace to walk up to him and say, 'Cal, I forgive you.' But I can hardly imagine it, let alone do it."

Nana clucked again. "Keep trying. You can't hate a man forever simply because he loved you too much."

Willow snorted. "He didn't love me. He was horny and he ruined my life."

"You know he loved you," Nana scolded. "Still does."

NANA'S WORDS echoed in Willow's head as she watched her friend Mick exchange vows with Tonya Green. Willow and Mick had been friends since high school. They'd even dated for a few months, B.C. Before Cal. But pretty soon they'd both realized they weren't happy as boyfriend and girlfriend, and they'd gone back to being platonic pals. She'd hung out with him a lot when Cal went away to college, after her freshman year.

Cal had been jealous, she recalled, though there was no reason for him to be.

Mick had struggled in recent years, trying to find himself. He'd dated literally dozens of girls while he sporadically took classes at the junior college. Then he'd gotten Tonya pregnant and, after a brief freak-out, he'd abruptly grown up.

Willow had been riding in Mick's car the day of the tornado. He'd been hashing things out with her, using her as a sounding board as he tried to come to terms with the big changes in his life. Then the storm had sent his car crashing off a bridge and into the swollen Coombes Creek.

Unlike Willow, Mick hadn't suffered any serious injuries, but the accident had forced him to set new priorities. Now he was looking forward to his new family life. She couldn't recall ever seeing him so happy.

As she moved through the reception line a little later, Nana walked behind her and whispered names into her ear.

"You know that one's Tonya, right?" Nana said.

"The frilly white dress and veil tipped me off." She gave Tonya a hug, then Mick.

"I finally know what you've been talking about all these years," Mick said.

"What?"

"You said I would know when I found my passion, that there wouldn't be any doubt. You were right. I'm where I'm supposed to be now."

Willow squeezed Mick's hand. "How's Amanda taking it?" Amanda was Mick's older sister, who'd been taking care of him since their mother died years ago. She'd been frustrated with his lack of direction, and downright distraught when she'd found out about Tonya's pregnancy.

"Amanda is delirious she's getting rid of me."

"Hey, I heard that," said the platinum blonde in a pale blue bridesmaid's dress, standing next to Mick. Identifying her was easy—no one else had hair that color. Amanda smiled and addressed Willow. "I'm going to miss him, strange as that may sound. Willow, you look great."

"I'll second that." A dark-haired man with a chiseled face stood next to Amanda, a possessive arm around her waist. He could be none other than Dr. Hudson Stack, one of the rescue workers who had pulled Willow from the submerged car. "A whole lot better than when I helped load you into the ambulance. You must have remarkable recuperative powers."

"I had good doctors," Willow said humbly. "Thank you again, Dr. Stack, for what you did."

"Call me Hudson, please. And this must be the lovely Clea Marsden."

Willow could certainly see what Amanda saw in Dr. Stack. Handsome, brave and charming. On vacation from his demanding job in Boston, he'd rented the lake house next door to Amanda. He'd fallen so hard for his neighbor that he'd returned to Boston just long enough to tender his resignation and put his house on the market.

The rest of the wedding reception passed in a blur. Willow sat at a table in the gussied-up VFW hall, her cheat sheets hidden under her purse and her grandmother there for backup, and she continued to put on a good show. She had a few panicked moments when "strangers" approached and she couldn't place them, but she was always able to gloss over the fact that their names weren't on the tip of her tongue.

When she wasn't busy studying clothes and jewelry and hair color, she kept tabs on a certain man in a gray suit with a red carnation in his lapel. She couldn't help noticing that he was dancing up a storm. A regular social butterfly. But he seemed to be avoiding her corner of the room, and that was all she cared about.

SHERRY HARDISON could cut a mean jitterbug, Cal Chandler thought as he twirled her across one of his hips, then the other, her gauzy skirt flying so high she almost showed her panties. Sherry was his boss's new wife, a fun-loving party girl with a mop of blond curls and a dazzling smile. A nurse from Dallas, she'd come to Cottonwood last fall to take care of Jonathan when he'd broken his leg. She'd had a hard time fitting in at first, but soon everyone was able to see beyond her fancy clothes and her fast sports car to the truly kind, gentle person she was. She and Jon had married at Christmas, as soon as he could walk down the aisle under his own power, and all the ranch employees were crazy about her. She brought them lemonade on hot days and remembered their birthdays and their kids' birthdays.

And, boy, could she dance. Cal had learned to dance in college, when he and all his dateless buddies hung out at the C&W bars and took swing lessons from curvaceous instructors wearing tight denim just so they could hold a pretty girl in their arms. He seldom got to show off his skills with a partner this good.

But as fun and nice and pretty as Sherry was, there was someone else he would rather be dancing with.

"Why don't you just ask her, instead of staring at her like a scolded puppy?" Sherry asked.

Cal groaned. "Is it that obvious?"

"Like an elephant having an allergy fit."

"I can't ask her. She would freeze me solid with one look."

"You two have a history, I take it?"

Since Sherry was relatively new in town, she wouldn't know all the ancient history. "We dated for almost four years, when she was still in high school."

"Your first love."

His only.

"What went wrong?" Sherry asked in her forthright way. Not nosy, just concerned. She was always trying to help people.

"Oh, I couldn't tell you. It's too embarrassing. But just ask around. Almost everybody knows about it."

"Now I'm intrigued."

Shoot, she was going to find out anyway. "Her parents caught us in, shall we say, a compromising position?"

He could tell Sherry was trying not to laugh. "And that's why you broke up?"

"Believe me, it was no laughing matter. Her folks went ballistic. She was supposed to go off to college in the fall—Stanford. But after 'the incident,' as it was referred to, they didn't let her go. They thought she would 'go wild' way out there in California."

Sherry looked confused. "Did she need their permission?"

"She needed them to pay for it. Stanford's not cheap.

Willow didn't have the funds to do it without their help. She had to live at home and go to junior college for a couple of years."

The song ended, and by silent, mutual agreement Sherry and Cal headed for the refreshment table. "And that's why you broke up?" Sherry asked as Cal filled a cup with punch for her.

"I ruined her life."

"Oh, and I suppose she had nothing to do with it?" Sherry scoffed.

"Well." This was the part Cal hated to admit. "It *was* my fault. I sort of pressured her into it. She wasn't ready, but I was older and I'd waited all this time for her to grow up, and I was facing the prospect of her running off to California, half a country away—"

"And you wanted to bond with her more closely."

"Yeah." He couldn't believe he was talking to his boss's wife about sex, but Sherry was really easy to talk to.

Jonathan sauntered over, putting an end to the conversation. "You gonna monopolize my wife all night, Chandler?"

Sometimes, Cal couldn't tell if Jonathan was kidding or not. He'd always been kind of serious, though Sherry's freewheeling style had loosened him up quite a bit.

Sherry just punched Jonathan in the arm. "Why would you care? You don't dance. And this young man…" She plucked the red carnation from Cal's buttonhole. "…can dance." Then she stuck the flower between her teeth and struck a flamenco dancer's pose.

Jonathan grinned and took his wife's arm. "Come on, Sherrita, I'll show you some dancing." As he dragged her off, Sherry looked at Cal and nodded toward Willow, as if to say, *Ask her.*

Well, hell, why not? What was the worst that could happen? Willow wouldn't make a scene, not at her friend's wedding.

WILLOW DRAINED the last of her punch from the glass and checked her watch. She was getting tired. Ever since her hospital stay, she had almost no stamina. But her grandmother was having a good time, dancing with the bride's grandfather, and Willow didn't want to be a wet blanket.

A shadow fell across the table. Willow looked up, and her breath caught in her throat. A handsome, tanned man with sun-streaked hair stood before her, somberfaced. Uh oh, no woman to anchor him to. And he wore the ubiquitous gray suit, though his broad shoulders filled it out much better than the average man.

Momentarily panicked, her gaze darted to his lapel. Thank goodness, no red carnation. She'd thought she was in trouble there for a minute. Still, she had no clue who this man was—only that he made her palms damp and her mouth dry.

Whoa. Get a grip, there, Willomena.

He flashed a dazzling smile, and Willow's heartbeat accelerated to hyperspeed. "Hi, Willow."

"H-hello." How could she not remember a guy as appealing as this? He had a rugged outdoorsy-ness about him that made her think of sunshine and fresh air—and a few less innocent thoughts, as well.

"It's good to see you. I heard about your accident."

"It's nice to see you, too." *Whoever you are.* "I'm

fine now. Except for the black eye." She reached up and touched her discolored eye self-consciously. Almost two weeks since the accident, the bright purple bruises had faded to green and yellow, which she'd mostly disguised with makeup. But her cover-up job wasn't perfect.

"I think you look beautiful."

Ohh, a flatterer. She'd better be careful with this one. She resisted the urge to flirt back. What if he was married? The husband of a good friend?

Could he be Jeff Hardison? Handsome, blond...

No matter who he was, she had no business entertaining *ideas*. She had work to do. Preparations to make. A brain to fix.

"Your grandmother told me you were recuperating at her house," the man said.

"Nana is spoiling me rotten." Just keep talking. Maybe she would figure it out.

"She always did. Do you...would you dance with me?"

The exhaustion Willow had felt moments earlier vanished like mist on a hot day. "Sure," she heard herself say. Oh, why not? It was just a dance. No law said she couldn't dance with a sexy guy at a wedding.

The song was an old number by Clint Black, and the man took Willow into his arms in an easy two-step. She didn't consider herself much of a dancer, but her partner was easy to follow and soon they were gliding across the floor with little effort, a veritable Fred and Ginger.

"So, what are you up to these days?" Willow asked. This question had served her well all evening. Once someone started talking about themselves, she could usually figure out who they were.

The man shrugged his broad shoulders. "Same old stuff. Making a living. Trying to stay out of trouble."

That was no help!

"I hear you're off to med school in a few weeks," he said.

"Mmm-hmm."

"You've worked pretty hard to get there. You must be proud."

"Still a lot of work ahead." More than anyone knew.

Willow didn't want to talk about herself, and her dance partner *wouldn't* talk about himself. So they danced in a highly charged silence, gliding across the floor in perfect harmony. The man's hands were large, slightly rough from hard work and unusually warm. The one at her waist felt like it could burn a hole through her silk dress.

She avoided looking straight at him because something in his eyes made her want to squirm uncomfortably. It was almost as if he knew more about her than she knew herself, that he could see deep to her core and know her innermost secrets.

But how could that be? This man could not possibly be someone she knew well or she would have figured out his identity by now. Although his voice struck a slight chord of familiarity, she couldn't place it. It was deep, a little bit hoarse and husky, as if he were just recovering from a cold or had been yelling too long and too loud at a baseball game.

The bouncy song came to a close, then immediately blended into a slow ballad, some dreamy old thing by Patsy Cline. Willow knew she should thank the man for the dance and sit down. A song like this was reserved for lovers, so they could hold each other close and murmur into each other's ears and be intimate in a public place.

She opened her mouth, but no words came out. Instead she nestled into the warm embrace of her mysterious stranger, where she seemed to fit perfectly. There wasn't even a moment of awkwardness. His strong arms slid around her waist, hers went around his neck and she laid her head lightly on his shoulder. She could smell traces of his aftershave, something old-fashioned like English Leather, or maybe just lime-scented shaving cream. She'd never been good at telling one smell apart from another, which was unfortunate, because smell was one of the main cues face-blind people used to distinguish friends…and lovers.

Mmm, she was sure she would remember this scent, though. Shampoo? Starch? Laundry detergent? Whatever it was, the blend was intoxicating.

Willow hoped no one was watching her. They might think it strange to see her so intimately wrapped up with—*whom?* Who could it be? Was she behaving inappropriately? Surely if the man was married he wouldn't act like this in public. But men could certainly be cads.

Oh, shoot, she didn't care. Anyway, the lights had been turned down so low, no one could see who was dancing with whom. An old-fashioned disco ball spun in the air above them, the tiny bits of mirrored glass casting glittering flecks of light over the dancers, creating a cocoon of surrealism.

Her partner had maneuvered her away from the main crowd on the floor, Willow realized. Spinning slowly through the song's smoky tendrils, they'd angled toward some ivy-festooned, papier-mâché Roman columns, then into a shadowy alcove. And there, behind a screen of ivy leaves, he kissed her.

Chapter Two

It was an amazing kiss, Willow thought dazedly as she sank into it, her bones turning to mush. Amazing as the kiss was, it was even more astonishing that she let him kiss her. She didn't offer even a token protest as his warm mouth closed over hers, tentatively at first, probably prepared for an objection. And when none came, his kiss became more sure as he took control of her mouth, as well as all her senses.

She'd never been kissed like this, as if the man were pouring his entire soul into one embrace. If his kiss was this intoxicating, what might it be like to actually—

She shut down that line of thought and dived headfirst into the kiss, living in the moment. That was something else she wasn't very good at. She was always thinking forward, planning ahead, worrying about all contingencies. But for this moment, she didn't worry. And it felt pretty darn good to just shed everything but the feel of the man's arms around her, his hands in her hair, and his amazing mouth caressing hers with such strength and gentleness at the same time, playing her the way a master musician would play even a run-of-the-mill violin and make it sing.

His curious fingers found the stitched cut on the side of her head, which she'd artfully hidden by combing her hair just right. She took his hand and pulled it away from her injury, suddenly self-conscious about it.

"I'm sorry," he murmured. "You're probably still tender there."

"It's not that. I just don't want you to know all my secrets." She rubbed her cheek against the slight roughness of his. "I worked hard to hide those stitches."

He slid his hand under her heavy hair around to the nape of her neck. "I want to know all your secrets."

Now she was getting embarrassed. She could feel her face flushing. This was all so…not like her. She didn't kiss strange men in public places.

"All I could think about, all night long, was kissing you," he tried again. "I know it's probably too much, too fast, but—"

She took his face between her hands, stood on her toes and kissed him again. She didn't want to talk yet. She didn't want mere words to pull her back into the real world.

He groaned low in his throat, wrapped his arms around her, as if sheltering her from prying eyes, and deepened the kiss for a few precious seconds before abruptly ending it.

He was breathing hard. Seemingly with some effort, he set her away from him. "Damn, darlin', that's some potent kiss you got there."

"Likewise." Willow wasn't a hundred percent in control of herself, even now when she wasn't wrapped in his arms.

"If we weren't here in the middle of the VFW hall—"

Willow covered her face. "Don't say it." Though it was true and she knew it. If they were in private, he wouldn't stop at a kiss. And she wouldn't want him to.

Her brain injury must have been more extensive than she thought. She was completely insane, certifiably!

"Sorry." He brushed a strand of hair from her cheek, tucked it behind her ear. "I didn't mean to overwhelm you. It's just that I've pictured this moment for such a long time—"

"You have?"

"I think about you a lot. Probably too much to be good for me."

Willow would have loved to be able to tell him she'd thought about him, too, that she'd noticed him, that she'd hoped he would ask her out or that she might be brave enough to ask him out.

But she hadn't thought about any guy in that way for a long time. Not since her sophomore year at University of Texas, when she'd finally been out from under her parents' control for the first time ever—and away from curious, small-town eyes. She'd gone a little bit wild, dating a whole slew of guys in some misguided effort to wipe memories of Cal Chandler out of her mind.

She'd been intrigued with some of them, and she'd tried her best to transform mild interest into wild attraction. But she'd never wanted any of them enough to sleep with them. Cal was the only one she'd ever loved enough to risk sex with, and look what a disaster that had turned into.

Then her class work had become more demanding, and she'd given up on guys altogether—with some relief. She was glad to not have to worry about sex anymore.

"This isn't how I wanted to start things with us, Willow."

She raised her eyebrows. "How did you want to start?"

"With a date. A nice, normal date. Could we do that? Could we start over?"

There were a zillion reasons for her to say no, starting with the fact she didn't know who he was. She had to get ready for her move to Dallas. She had to unscramble her brains.

But there was one, overriding reason to say yes. That kiss. She'd never experienced anything like it. Not even Cal's kisses, much as she'd loved him, had made her want to rip off her clothes and offer herself like some pagan sacrifice. What if this was the sort of chemistry that happened only once in a lifetime? Could she just walk away from that?

"I'm moving to Dallas in five weeks," she said. "You do understand that, right?"

"Willow. You don't always have to think about what happens five weeks from now. Or even one week from now. How about just thinking through tomorrow? Going out to dinner with me. Just a simple date."

Well, when he put it that way… "Okay," she heard herself saying.

"I'll pick you up at your grandmother's at seven. We'll go to the Party Barge."

"Sounds fun." Willow suppressed the giddy laughter that threatened. The Party Barge. It was a big barge that cruised Town Lake on weekends. Patrons dressed up, ate prime rib and danced to live big-band music. When she'd been in high school, she and Cal had talked about going there for her twenty-first birthday, when she could legally order a cocktail. It had seemed an impossibly sophisticated and expensive evening out for a couple of dreamy kids.

Well, her twenty-first birthday had come and gone a long time ago, and she'd never been to the Party Barge.

Suddenly, Willow realized she was standing behind the ivy curtain all alone. Her mystery man had vanished while she'd been momentarily lost in her adolescent fantasy. That's what she got for thinking about Cal when she'd had a flesh-and-blood man within reach.

She checked to be sure her clothes were in order— that she'd ripped them off only in her imagination—then slipped out of the sheltered alcove. No one seemed to be paying her any mind, thank heavens. She made a bee-line for the bathroom, where she straightened her hair and wiped off her smeared lipstick. Her face was still flushed, her eyes a little brighter than usual, but probably no one would notice that.

Suddenly, her fatigue caught up with her again. She'd definitely overdone it today. This was her first real outing since coming home from the hospital. The surge of adrenaline brought on by the dance and kiss had dwindled, leaving her feeling a bit washed-out.

She would find Nana and go home, where she could sit quietly and think about her date tomorrow. She was pretty sure that was all she would be able to think about.

Nana was sitting at their table, fanning herself with a paper fan she kept folded in her purse. She looked up when Willow approached.

"Oh, there you are. I wondered where you'd got to. Are you about ready to go?"

"I was just going to ask you the same thing." Willow picked up her purse and tucked her cheat sheet index cards inside. She would throw them away when she got home. Once everyone changed clothes, they would be useless and she would have to start over.

"Oh, dear, you're feeling all right, aren't you?" Nana asked, concern wrinkling her brow. "You look a little flushed."

Leave it to Nana, with her eagle eyes, to notice. "I'm fine. It's a little warm in here. Um, Nana, did you happen to notice who I was dancing with a little while ago?"

Nana's eyes sparkled mischievously. "No. Who was it?"

Willow groaned. "I was hoping you'd tell me. Are you sure you didn't see? We were dancing to Patsy Cline."

"A slow song, huh?" Nana was clearly amused.

"This isn't funny. I told him I'd go out with him, and then I…" She lowered her voice to a whisper. "I kissed him. And I don't know who he is."

Nana shrugged helplessly. "I'm sorry, sweetheart. I was doing a bit of dancing myself and I guess I just lost track of you. So you're going on a date with him? When? Where's he taking you?"

"Tomorrow, the Party Barge. Oh, Nana, what if he's someone totally inappropriate? Someone I'd never in a million years go out with? What if he's married or dating one of my friends?"

"Then he would try to see you on the sly. He wouldn't take you out on a date and certainly not to such a public place."

Nana had a point.

"You're worrying for nothing." Nana patted Willow's arm as they headed for the exit. The bride and groom had already left for their honeymoon. Willow supposed there were people she should say goodnight to, but she would have to summon up names again and she really didn't have the energy. So she just waved at anyone who made eye contact.

Soon they were safely in Nana's car, a twenty-year-old Ford Taurus she kept in immaculate condition.

"Cottonwood is full of nice young men," Nana said as she pulled out of the parking lot. "Maybe your mystery man was that nice sheriff's deputy, Luke Rheems. He's handsome and eligible and I noticed him watching you."

"Or he might have been Orville, the garbage man."

"I think you would have noticed if he was missing several teeth. Anyway, he was young, wasn't he?"

Willow shrugged. "Age is one of those qualities I have trouble with. I can tell a child from an old man, but those ages in between tend to look a lot alike. Oh, Nana, what if he's someone I have nothing in common with?"

"You won't know until you spend time with him."

"How can I go out with a man," Willow tried again, "if I don't know his name?"

That stumped Nana for a moment. Then she got a decisive look on her face. "This isn't a problem. When he comes to pick you up tomorrow, I'll be there to greet him. Before you leave, I'll have a private word with you and I'll tell you who he is. Then you'll at least be able to call him by his name."

"What if *you* don't know him?"

"Then he'll introduce himself and the problem will

be solved another way. Willow, darling, you spend way too much time worrying. It will all work out. I mean, what's the worst that could happen? You admit to him that you have a bit of a problem recognizing faces—"

"No! I can't tell him that. I can't tell anyone that. Then it would get all over town, and people would feel sorry for me even as they're avoiding me—"

"Oh, Willow," Nana said. "Like I said, you worry too much."

CAL WAS MORE NERVOUS about his date with Willow than he could ever remember being. He still couldn't believe she'd agreed to go out with him. Or that he'd kissed her. Or that she'd kissed him back.

And what a kiss. It wasn't like he remembered from five years ago. He'd always enjoyed kissing Willow, of course. She'd been shy about it at first, very inexperienced. She'd confessed that he was only the third boy she'd ever kissed, and the first two had been just little pecks. But he'd persevered, and pretty soon they were making out every chance they got—any time they could escape the watchful eyes of her overprotective parents.

He'd been crazy for her, just about as horny as an eighteen-year-old boy could get. But he'd never gotten the idea that Willow was similarly inflamed. She went through the motions and her technique improved. But Cal never sensed that she was getting carried away.

Last night at the wedding, however, had been a whole 'nother story. The woman had been on fire, just as he'd been. Maybe that was the difference between the girl he'd fallen in love with and the woman she'd become. The girl had kissed him because she loved him and wanted to please him. The woman had kissed him because she'd wanted to.

He wondered what else about Willow had changed. She was taller and she'd filled out slightly, though she still had that reed-slim body and waist-length hair that haunted his dreams. But had she changed inside? Could he push his outdated memories of Willow into the past where they belonged and fall in love with the woman she'd become?

He looked forward to finding out.

Her grandmother's house looked the same as it always did when he pulled up out front. The large, two-story frame house, almost a hundred years old, had a wide, inviting front porch with a swing. The front yard was practically overrun with roses in every color, blooming like crazy. Willow had grown up in Mooresville, on the other side of Town Lake. Her parents owned the bank there, and they both worked there full-time. So Willow had spent summers living with Clea.

Clea Marsden was the perfect grandmother. She baked cookies and made fresh lemonade and sewed quilts and grew roses. But she was a modern thinker and a lot more liberal than Willow's parents. While Willow's parents had disapproved of her romance with Cal because of the age difference, Clea had encouraged it. She'd told Cal once that she could tell from the very beginning that the two of them belonged together. So Cal had run tame at Clea's big, homey house all summer long.

Even after Willow had broken up with him, Cal had stayed close to Clea. He did odd jobs for her now, fixing little things around the house, checking the oil and tire pressure in her car, mowing the lawn. She'd been a

widow for a long time, and she was pretty self-suffi-
cient, but everyone needed help now and then.

Now it was seven o'clock on the nose. Willow had
always valued punctuality, so Cal had made sure he
wouldn't be late. With one final glance in the rearview
mirror, he got out and headed for the door, his stomach
tumbling with nerves. Those weren't butterflies in there;
it felt more like a herd of rhinoceros.

He rang the bell. Heard footsteps. Swallowed, his
mouth suddenly full of cotton. The door opened, and
Clea stood there, a pleasant, welcoming smile on her
face. Her smile faltered a moment when she recognized
Cal, but then it returned, even bigger than before. Had
Willow not told her grandmother to expect him?

"Come in, come in, Cal. It's so good to see you. Willow's just finishing her hair—she'll be down in a minute." She showed him into the living room, where a
plate of cookies sat invitingly on the coffee table.
"Would you like a cookie?"

Cal groaned. "Are those your oatmeal peanut-butter
cookies?"

"Mmm-hmm. Just baked them this afternoon."

"I don't want to spoil my—okay, just one." He
couldn't resist. He took a cookie and bit into it, savoring the sweet, rich taste that brought back a thousand
memories. He and Willow used to pack picnic lunches
and hike into the woods that ran through the back of the
Hardison Ranch. They would spread out a quilt by the
creek, gorge themselves on fried chicken and potato
salad and at least half a dozen cookies each, then swim
in the creek.

Clea disappeared briefly, and when she returned, she

had her purse in her hand. "I hope you won't think I'm rude, but I have bingo tonight. You kids have fun!" She waved and disappeared again. Moments later, Cal heard the back door open and close.

Less than a minute after Clea's departure, Cal heard another door open and close, then footsteps coming down the stairs.

He bounced to his feet just as Willow entered the living room. She looked like a goddess in a white gauzy summer dress. It wasn't short or clingy or low-cut, but Cal found it sexy as hell, the way it gently conformed to her breasts and the curve of her hip. Her dainty feet were encased in high-heeled white sandals, and she'd woven her long hair up into a sophisticated twist of some kind.

"Hi," she said with a shy smile.

"Hi, yourself. You look gorgeous."

She looked around. "Where's Nana?"

"Oh, she said she had to go to bingo."

A look of panic overtook Willow's face. "What? You mean she's gone?"

"Yeah. Is something wrong?"

Willow headed for the kitchen. Cal followed, curious as to why her grandmother's departure would upset Willow. Was Clea in ill health? Willow opened the back door, stared out, then slowly shut it. She turned toward Cal, looking very upset indeed.

"You're right. She's gone. Bingo? I didn't know the church had bingo on Sunday nights."

"She could have gone somewhere else. The Elks Lodge, maybe. Willow, is something wrong?"

Willow seemed to pull herself together. "No. I just didn't realize she was leaving, that's all. She surprised me."

Apparently so.

"We should probably go," Cal said. "I don't want to miss boarding."

WILLOW COULD NOT believe her grandmother had run out on her like that. Had she forgotten she had an important mission? How was Willow supposed to go out on a date with a man when she didn't know his name?

Well, she supposed if her mystery date were a known ax murderer or recently released from the mental hospital, Nana would have said something. Unless he did away with Nana while Willow was primping....

Now she was being paranoid. Willow supposed it was safe to go out with him. But how could Nana have forgotten to tell Willow who he was?

Was Nana getting senile? Something else to worry about.

She would try very hard to put her worries out of her head for now, however. She was going out dining and dancing with a handsome—at least, she thought he was handsome—man, and she was going to enjoy it. She decided to assign him a fictitious name, just until she discovered what his real one was.

Let's see. Bill? Fred? No, those weren't right.

Hank. She would think of him as Hank.

"Just let me get my purse and I'll be ready."

Hank drove a truck, she soon discovered. An old brown Chevy, sturdy and utilitarian, recently waxed and immaculate inside. He helped her into the high seat, his gaze lingering on her leg when her dress rode up a few inches. She gave him a look that let him know she'd caught him, but at the same time, his frank interest caused something to ignite deep inside her.

Oh, Lord, it was too early in the evening to deal with *those* kinds of feelings. She had to keep her wits about her, be alert for any sort of clue to her date's identity.

His job. She would ask him about his work. "So, how is your work going these days?"

"I'm off for a couple of weeks. I don't know if you heard, but that tornado knocked me around a bit, too. I didn't have the sense to get out of my truck and find cover when the sirens went off. But, you know, we get so many warnings that never amount to anything, I just wasn't worried when I should have been."

"I know. Mick was sure we could make it home before the storm hit. I hope you weren't seriously injured."

"I got sucked right out of my truck, then pinned under it."

"Oh, my God, I'm surprised you're walking around." Willow tried to remember whether she'd heard of any other serious injuries. But those first few days after her accident, she'd been so focused on her own recovery she hadn't thought much about others' misfortunes. And if she had heard about this man's injuries, she probably wouldn't remember, she thought grimly. Her week in the hospital was mostly a blur.

"I broke some ribs, punctured a lung," he said, as if that were no big deal. "It could have been bad, 'cause the ambulances couldn't get through, but Dr. Stack came along. He knew what to do."

"That guy gets around. He helped rescue me, too."

"Anyway, Jon gave me a couple of weeks off to recuperate. He also loaned me this truck, until I can get mine replaced."

John Who? Willow wondered. She decided to go out on a limb. "You mean Jon Hardison?"

"Yeah. That's where I'm working now."

Willow's breath caught in her throat. The Hardison Ranch was where Cal worked, last she'd heard. It was on the tip of her tongue to ask "Hank" if he knew Cal, which of course he would, but she stopped herself. She did not want to be one of those tedious women who talk incessantly about old boyfriends they hadn't quite gotten over.

Anyway, she'd gotten over Cal. Completely.

All right, so her mystery man was a ranch hand. Nothing wrong with that.

"It's good, honest work," Hank said, almost as if he'd heard her. "I thought I'd do it just temporary, but I found I like it. Well, not all of it. Castrating calves and putting up fences and hauling hay—that's just work. But I like hanging out with horses and cows. And I seem to be pretty good at it. In fact, Wade's got me over at his place half the time, working with the green horses. I got to show some of his campers how I halter-train a colt once. That was a hoot."

Wade was Jonathan's younger brother, a national rodeo champion. He'd started a horse-breeding operation on his portion of the ranch, and he also ran a rodeo camp for city kids, which was gaining a national reputation.

Willow smiled at the image of "Hank" working with the kids. Oh, she was liking him more and more. What wasn't to like about a guy who had an affinity for animals and kids?

Cal was kind to animals, she reflected. She'd always admired him for that. She'd been so proud of him when he'd gotten accepted into vet school. Not that anyone had been surprised. Cal was so smart, a straight-A student without even trying. The surprise had come when he'd dropped out after a year. And while it didn't bother her at all that "Hank" worked on a ranch, because he was obviously suited to it, it seemed like a huge waste that someone with Cal's intellect and abilities, and enough family money to pursue any endeavor in the world, chose menial labor.

Oh, hell, here she was thinking about Cal again.

"I didn't mean to go on and on," Hank said apologetically. "My work might not be glamorous, but it's worthwhile. I wanted you to know that."

"I have no problem with your work," she said, bemused. Did he think she was a total snob, that she wouldn't be seen with someone who didn't drive a Mercedes and wear a tie every day?

"I want to talk about you," he said.

"Nothing about me is very interesting." Besides, if they focused on her, she would *never* find out who he was.

"I beg to differ." He gave her a smoldering look that could have set her panties on fire. *Oh, come on.* What was wrong with her that she reacted so strongly?

He must not be a stranger, she reasoned. Her subconscious must know this man. That was the only way she could explain her strong sexual response to him.

They parked in the lot, got their reserved tickets at a booth, then stood in line at the dock to board the gleaming white barge. The sun was still out, and it was warm. She hoped they wouldn't have to stand in the heat for long.

Hank immediately sensed her discomfort. "Why don't we sit at one of those picnic tables in the shade?" he suggested. "We've got our tickets. We don't really have to stand in line."

"But I want a good table," she argued. "I've fantasized about doing this for years. I want it to be perfect."

Hank winked. "I know the maître d'. Our table is reserved."

Just then the gangway was opened and everyone started boarding, so they remained in line. Hank and the maître d', whose nametag identified him as Ken, shook hands and did a little backslapping. Willow listened attentively in case Ken used Hank's real name, but he didn't, darn it. They were shown to a lovely table for two, tucked away in a private corner. But they had a good view out their own little porthole.

"Oh, this is perfect," Willow said.

And it was, every nuance of the evening. As the barge got under way, beginning its languorous journey around the glass-smooth lake, Hank ordered some expensive French burgundy. Willow was only sorry she didn't know enough about wine to fully appreciate it, but it tasted wonderful and she didn't object when Hank refilled her glass.

She sipped slowly, savoring the deep, dark flavor. Every bite of her tender prime rib melted in her mouth.

And of course they danced. Hank was a really good dancer—not flashy, not a show-off. Just smooth. Her heart felt like a balloon inflating in her chest every time the band started up a slow song.

He pulled the same trick as he had at the wedding reception, dancing her into the shadows. But instead of pulling her more tightly into his arms and kissing her, he guided her out the hatch and onto the deck.

The deck was almost deserted. They found a secluded portion of railing and leaned against it, watching the shoreline slip by as the flaming sun settled behind a distant hill.

"It's so pretty out here," Willow said on a sigh. "I tend to take the lake for granted. I know it's here, I cross over the bridge every time I go to my parents' house. But I don't think much about it."

"It'd be nice to have a little sailboat out here," Hank said. "With just the sound of the wind and the lapping water, you could really think. Clear all the junk out of your head."

"And what sort of junk would a man like you have to clear out?"

"Oh, you know. Baggage. Bad habits. Regrets."

"Surely you don't have many of those."

"Only one, darlin'." And then he kissed her, and she didn't resist at all.

This really wasn't like her, she thought yet again as she returned his kiss in full measure, their tongues dancing, her breath rising and falling in tandem with his. His hand brushed against her breast, almost as if by accident. He did it again, turning the incidental contact into a tender caress. Her nipples hardened, thrusting against the silk and lace of her bra, the sensation so intense it was almost painful.

The assault on her senses was so overwhelming she had to put a stop to the embrace. If she didn't, she was afraid what might happen. With determination, she pulled away, pushing slightly against his shoulders for good measure.

The effect was like a bucket of cold water. Hank looked so crestfallen, she wanted to take it back, to return to his embrace and just let him do whatever he wanted.

"Willow, I'm sorry. Please, don't be mad. You're just so beautiful tonight, I can't hardly control myself." His words came in an urgent whisper, even huskier than usual. "I'll be good. I will. The last—the very last thing I want to do is rush you."

Good heavens, didn't he get it? She wanted to be rushed. She wasn't upset about his behavior, only a bit bewildered by her own. The last thing she needed was an apology. How could a man apologize for making her feel so special, so excited, like a top just before someone pulled the string and sent it spinning out of control?

"Will the cruise be over soon?" Her own voice sounded a bit hoarse.

He wouldn't meet her gaze. "Guess that means you *are* mad."

"No. I just—I'd like to be alone. With you, I mean. Alone with you."

Chapter Three

Cal was sure he was dreaming. He'd counted himself lucky that Willow didn't throw things at him when he approached her at Mick and Tonya's wedding. He'd thought divine intervention must have been responsible when she let him kiss her the first time, and when she'd agreed to go out with him, he'd thought he must be the luckiest man in the world.

But he'd never dreamed he would hear those words out of Willow's mouth, not on their first date in five years. *I'd like to be alone...alone with you.* Yup. Had to be a dream.

If it was, he hoped he never woke up.

The Party Barge was about to dock. Cal left a generous tip for their server, then steered Willow toward the gangway. They were first in line to get off.

"You're not getting too tired, are you?" He was still a little shaky from his own hospital stay, and he'd been released several days before Willow.

"No, I'm fine. And the Party Barge was wonderful, everything I always imagined it would be. But I'm ready to—"

She stopped, and Cal was dying to know what she was about to say. But he didn't want to push her. He again helped her into the truck, then climbed in and started the engine.

"Where do you want to go?" he asked as he eased the truck out of the bumpy parking lot, glad they were beating the crowd. "We could take a drive. Lots of pretty country roads around here." Though he would not go anywhere near the place where he and Willow used to go parking.

"Could we go to your place?" She sounded a little nervous. "Or maybe it's rude to just invite myself over. You could— I mean, Nana wouldn't mind if we hung out at her house. But you might not think hanging with my grandmother is that cool." She laughed, then looked at him uncertainly to see if he was laughing with her.

He smiled. She *was* nervous. "We can definitely go to my house." He wasn't the best housekeeper in the world, but he hired a cleaning service to come in every couple of weeks and give the place a good going-over. Fortunately, they'd just come that morning. "Not that I don't adore Clea, and I wouldn't mind a few more of her cookies."

"They're outrageously good, aren't they? You should try her fudge."

It was on the tip of Cal's tongue to remind Willow that he *had* tried Clea's fudge dozens, maybe hundreds of times. They were his favorite, and Willow used to accuse him of dating her just so he could get to her grandmother's cookies.

It was odd Willow wouldn't remember that. But he decided to say nothing. He didn't want to bring up the past at all. They were starting over tonight with a clean slate.

Cal rented an apartment in one of Cottonwood's oldest neighborhoods, just off the square, on the second floor of a painted-lady Victorian.

His grandmother on his mother's side had left him a farm up in Lancaster, a small town just southwest of Dallas. He could have sold it and used the money to buy just about any kind of house he wanted. But buying seemed like such a permanent decision for someone who didn't know where he would be in five years. So he rented, and the money he collected from leasing the farm for grazing went into shares of a mutual fund that had performed steadily despite the roller-coaster economy. If Cal ever decided what he wanted to be when he grew up, he had the funds to do it.

That was a big *if.*

"Oh, my gosh, what a great place," Willow said when he turned into the driveway. "I've always loved this house. The Whittakers used to live here, didn't they?"

"They still do—on the ground floor. They rent out the second floor to me." He took her around to the back and up the fire-escape stairs. They could have gone in the front door, but Mr. and Mrs. Whittaker would waylay them and talk their ears off, and he would *never* get Willow alone.

He unlocked the French doors that led from the balcony into the living room. Before he could switch the lights on, a familiar black-and-white blur met them, tail thumping, pink tongue lolling.

"Oh, a dog!" Willow stooped down to pet the border collie. "Hi there, fella."

"It's a girl."

"Oh, sorry. What's her name?"

"Clementine. Clem for short."

"She certainly is well-behaved."

"She likes to please. Clem, go outside." The dog reluctantly but obediently slipped out the door and down the stairs.

"Aren't you afraid she'll run off?" Willow asked. "You don't have a fence."

"No, she won't go anywhere. She's trained. Besides, she knows she's got a good deal here. Have a seat." He switched on a couple of lights. He didn't want Willow to think he had seduction in mind.

And he didn't. Okay, it was in his mind, but he had no intentions of following through. His raging hormones had driven Willow away from him once. He had to prove that he was attracted to more than just her delectable body. Not that he had any complaints about the package.

"Do you want some coffee?" he asked, playing the polite host. Coffee would keep their hands and their mouths busy. They could listen to music. Watch a DVD. Play checkers.

"That sounds good."

He was a patient man, he thought as he left her for the kitchen. He'd waited five years to make Willow his again. He could wait a little longer.

He'd just turned on the coffee maker when an ear-piercing scream split the evening calm. Cal raced back to the living room, visions of mayhem and blood making his pulse pound. He found Willow standing on the sofa, her eyes huge, her face pale as vanilla ice cream. She pointed down to the rug near a chair.

"I just saw the biggest rat in the entire world. It went under that chair." She pointed more emphatically.

Cal groaned. "Oh, no. Willow, it's okay. It's just Rudy."

"You name your rats?" She didn't budge from her position on the couch.

"Rudy is a ferret." Cal got down on his hands and knees and peered under the recliner. Two red eyes glowed at him. "You probably scared him more than he scared you."

"I seriously doubt that."

Cal reached under the chair and withdrew the cream-colored ferret. Rudy was trembling, but with a few strokes and some reassuring words from Cal, he soon calmed down.

The same couldn't be said for Willow.

"I'm sorry he scared you," Cal said. "He's supposed to be in his cage, but he's figured out how to escape. He squeezes under the door, I think." Turning to his ferret, he scratched it under its chin. "Aren't you a smart fellow?"

Willow looked at him dubiously from where she still perched on top of the sofa.

"Come down from there. Rudy is completely harmless, I promise."

She stepped down to the floor using his hand for support, then sank onto the sofa. "Sorry about that. Guess I just proved the stereotype. I screamed like a girlie-girl, didn't I?"

Cal laughed. "You did."

She cast a cautious look toward the ferret, which had climbed onto Cal's shoulder and was staring back just as hard at Willow. "Okay, let's have a look at Rudy."

Cal scooped Rudy off his shoulder and held him out to Willow. She lightly stroked his head. And when he seemed to enjoy her attention, she took him into her lap.

"Well, I guess you're pretty cute. Not really *that* much like a rat."

This was the Willow he remembered. Cal had always maintained a menagerie at the little farm just outside town where he'd grown up, and Willow had always loved the animals. She only objected a little when he tried to make a pet out of a giant king snake he'd found in the garage.

Clem yipped once to be let in. And right after that, two more members of his household darted into the living room, probably curious about the screaming. The two cats hopped up on the sofa, eager to make the newcomer's acquaintance.

"Goodness, are there more?" Willow asked.

"The orange one is October. The black-and-white one is Tyson." Time enough later to tell her about the other members of his family, not all of which were cute and cuddly.

Willow scratched each of the cats, showing a bit of extra attention to Tyson's left ear. Half of it was missing. "These guys look pretty battle-scarred."

"They're shelter cats. Wild as March hares when I got them."

"They're tame enough now." Both cats were vying for Willow's attention, trying to climb into her lap with the ferret. "Wait a minute. How come they don't try to eat the ferret?"

Cal shrugged. "They know it's not allowed. You have to have rules." Unfortunately. he wanted to throw away the rules when it came to Willow. "October, Tyson, that's enough."

Both cats froze and looked at Cal.

"You heard me. Scat."

They left Willow's lap and sauntered away. Willow stared after them in amazement. "I never saw cats mind like that before."

Again, Cal shrugged. "You can teach them things if you're patient. You just have to learn how to think like a cat." He picked up Rudy from Willow's lap. The ferret squeaked in protest. He'd taken an instant liking to Willow, once he'd recovered from the fright of her screaming. "I'll put him up. The coffee should be ready in a minute."

WILLOW WATCHED as he exited the living room, the ferret slung casually over his shoulder. Her still-nameless date had the cutest butt she'd ever seen, even in a pair of oatmeal-colored dress trousers. She wondered what he would look like in snug, faded Levi's, and the thought made her light-headed.

She hadn't pegged him for an animal lover. Most of the cowboys she'd known over the years—and there were plenty in Cottonwood—thought of animals as commodities. Oh, they might have a slight thing for their horses. But cats and dogs and ferrets? It was like *Wild Kingdom* around here.

Cal had loved animals, too, she recalled. He'd taken in as many strays of all stripes as his mother would tolerate. That was why she always thought he would be such an excellent vet, like his father and grandfather before him. That was why she'd been so shocked and disappointed when she'd heard he dropped out of vet school.

It was an odd coincidence that Hank was an animal

lover, too. She just must be attracted to that type of man, she reasoned. If there was an animal-lover gene, maybe she subconsciously recognized it and was attracted to the kindness that went along with it. She liked a strong, macho man as well as any girl, but she wouldn't tolerate strength without a dash of kindness, too.

A man who was gentle and patient with animals would probably be a good father.

She sat up straighter as her skin prickled with awareness. Where had that thought come from? She wasn't shopping for the future father of her children. Marriage and parenthood weren't compatible with med school. They would be *years* down the line for her. It was especially inappropriate for her to be thinking those thoughts in connection with a man whose name she didn't know.

This situation had gotten totally ridiculous. Maybe there was a clue here in his apartment....

She stood up and looked around for some stray mail, a magazine, maybe. But the only magazine she saw was *TV Guide*, and there was no address label.

She sighed. He was going to get suspicious if she called him "Hey, you."

Hank returned a few moments later. "You want cream in your coffee?"

"No, black is fine." She'd learned to drink it like that in college, pulling all-nighters when she literally didn't have enough money for cream. Truthfully, she didn't really want coffee right now.

She wanted Hank.

He brought her coffee in a thick, blue ceramic mug, then sat next to her, close but not touching. She blew on the coffee to cool it and took a sip. "Good."

"Do you want to watch a movie?"

Only if we watch it while we're making love.

The thought shocked her. When had she become so wanton? She wasn't even sure she would like sex. Her one and only experience with it had been so horrible that for a long time she thought maybe she should just become a nun or a hermit.

But her hormones insisted that making love with Hank would definitely not be unpleasant. Quite the contrary. She could tell just by watching him that he would be slow and gentle, patient with her clumsy efforts, seeing to her comfort and pleasure before his own. Just as he could gentle a wild stray cat, he would calm her skittishness.

The silence had stretched uncomfortably. Willow knew she needed to tame her wayward thoughts before she said or did anything foolish. Her hormones were completely 'round the bend.

"Do you want to watch TV?" he tried again.

No. That was something staid married couples did because they were bored with each other. She wanted to rip off that starched blue-gray shirt and see what his bare chest looked like. "Sure." Since her injury she found TV almost intolerable, since everyone had the same face. The few times she'd tried it, she'd been hopelessly confused.

They both leaned forward and reached for the *TV Guide* sitting on the coffee table. They collided, and half of Willow's coffee sloshed out of her cup and onto her thigh. She cried out more in surprise than in pain; the coffee wasn't that hot.

"Oh, my God, I'm sorry," Hank said, jumping to his feet. "Are you okay?"

"I'm fine, I just—"

"Your dress. It's not ruined, is it?" He dragged her toward the kitchen. "Let's rinse out the stain before it sets." Once in the kitchen, he stuck a dishcloth under the cold water, then began daubing at the spot on her dress, which was perilously close to…well, to where he shouldn't be touching.

Her body responded immediately, starting with a fireball between her legs that grew and radiated outward. Her breasts ached and felt too heavy, her insides quivered and her legs trembled. She leaned on the kitchen counter for support even as she closed her eyes and desperately wished that he would move his hand just a couple of inches to the left—

"Willow?"

She opened her eyes and saw Hank peering at her, concerned. But almost immediately his expression changed to one that more closely mirrored her own feelings. He'd seen the naked hunger in her face, in her eyes, and she feared—and hoped—he'd read her every lascivious thought.

And then she was in his arms and he was kissing her like he wanted to devour her, hot, demanding, commanding kisses, on her mouth and along her jaw and down her neck, his lips trailing fire wherever they went.

The comb fell out of her hair and the heavy mass tumbled down, making her feel even more wanton, like a virgin preparing for sacrifice. Not that this was any big sacrifice on her part. She'd wanted this from the moment this man had first taken her into his arms on the dance floor at the VFW Hall. Maybe she hadn't consciously been aware that was what she wanted, but her body had known. Her body had been absolutely certain.

Willow wrapped her arms around Hank and buried her fingers in his hair. She would have melted into him if she could have, merged herself with him; that was how keen her craving for him was.

Finally, she understood everything. She understood the craziness that made some of her girlfriends go completely nuts for a guy, put up with being treated like dirt, or completely forget the rules of safe conduct. She understood taking a risk, fighting anything that got in a woman's way.

It was for this, this feeling. A sensation that felt as if she were a soap bubble in the wind, about to burst.

"Willow." Her name on his lips was more of a groan. "I didn't mean for this to happen. I swear."

She knew that. She knew he had more on his mind than conquest. It had been her idea to come home with him, after all. She was the one who'd said she wanted to be alone with him. But her brain was short-circuiting, sending sparks everywhere in her body. She found it difficult to perform the mundane task of forming words.

But she wasn't interested in words anyway. She pulled his shirttail out from his pants and shoved her hands inside, next to his skin. Oh, yeah. Smooth and warm, just like she'd thought it would be. Rock-hard muscles covered with velvet smooth skin.

Was he tan all over, like his face and hands? Did he sometimes work without a shirt, all hot and sweaty?

The thought almost made her swoon.

"Willow …"

"I want you, Ha—" She stopped herself just before

she called him by the fictitious name she'd given him. How in the world would she explain that? He would think she'd gotten him confused with an old boyfriend.

"What?"

"I want your…your hands on me," she improvised, though he was already touching her everywhere, caressing her breasts through her dress, squeezing her bottom. She could feel his arousal pressing against her pelvis, and her body twitched as her imagination conjured up an image of him inside her.

Surely it wouldn't hurt, like it had before. The time she'd made love with Cal, she hadn't been ready. She hadn't been aroused because she didn't even know what arousal was. She'd been tense and terrified, a little girl in a woman's body who hadn't been ready for sex.

She was ready now. She was past ready.

He worked the zipper of her dress down her back and slid his hands inside, doing exactly what she was doing to him. She knew that once clothes started to come off, it would be very hard to change her mind about this.

She wouldn't change her mind. For whatever reason, this felt right to her. As if her body had been waiting her whole life to find this man. Maybe those were her hormones talking, rationalizing her outrageous behavior, but she didn't care. She was entitled to act like a crazy fool once in her life.

"Willow." Now her name sounded like a plea. "I feel like I'm rushing you."

"You're not."

"We could wait—"

"I don't want to wait." Willow knew she needed to explain herself. So she pulled herself together long enough so that she could string a few coherent sentences together. "A couple of weeks ago, I almost died. You could have, too. If that experience has taught us anything, shouldn't it be that we don't know what the future will bring? Sometimes it doesn't matter how carefully we plan for something or how cautious we are, it can all get screwed up in a heartbeat."

"Oh, Willow." He hugged her to him. "Nothing's going to happen to us."

"I'm sure you're right."

"We don't have to rush."

"We don't have to wait," she countered. If they waited, by tomorrow her sensible self might return and nix the whole thing. She simply couldn't bear that thought.

"Are you sure?"

She nodded, her eyes inexplicably moistening. Then she kissed him, pouring her heart and soul into the kiss. She felt like she'd known him forever. She'd always pooh-poohed the notion of soul mates, her scientific mind rejecting a notion that couldn't be measured or proven. But if soul mates existed, she suspected she had found hers.

She didn't need to know his name. She didn't need to recognize his face. She knew this man on a deeper, elemental level.

Still locked in a kiss, Hank scooped her up in his arms and carried her out of the kitchen. She thought they were going to the bedroom, but they didn't make it that far. He stopped near the sofa and set her down.

Her dress was already half falling off. She shrugged out of it, and it pooled at her feet. She noticed, in a detached sort of way, how odd it was to be standing in a man's apartment in nothing but her underthings. But she wasn't embarrassed. The strangeness of it felt stimulating.

She shivered.

"Are you cold?"

Cold was the furthest thing from her mind. "No. Don't stop."

He nuzzled her neck as he unhooked her bra, struggling briefly with the fastener. She was glad he hadn't just flicked it open one-handed. She liked to think that he hadn't unfastened hundreds of girls' bras before her. Of course, he would have more experience than her. Everyone did. Still, she wanted their lovemaking to be novel for him, as well as her.

Her bra landed on the floor. Then everything below her waist—slip, stockings, panties—were whisked down her legs. He pushed her onto the sofa so he could pull off her shoes, too. And she was gloriously naked with only her long hair to cover her, like Lady Godiva.

Not that she wanted to cover herself. Hank's frank visual perusal of her body was like turning the heat up on the stove. He yanked his shirt the rest of the way off. Belt, pants, boxers, shoes, all dispensed with just as efficiently as he'd gotten rid of her clothes.

Oh, he was beautiful. Tan all over except around his hips. Just a little bit of blond, curly hair on his chest forming a rough diamond between his flat, brown nipples. And a scar near the center of his chest, still red and puckered.

Then she looked lower, at the evidence of his arousal, and she was glad she was sitting down because she really did feel faint. She wanted to touch him, to see how really hard he was, to feel him pulsing with desire. She settled for holding out her hand to him, beckoning him to lie with her on the sofa.

"I have to get something first." He surprised her by turning and walking away. For the second time that evening she watched his butt as he exited the living room. Only this time it was a naked butt, and all she could do was sigh. In a few moments, those buns of steel would be hers, all hers. She quivered again.

He returned mere seconds later and set something on the floor by the sofa. Willow realized he'd gotten protection and felt even better about him. She hadn't even *thought* of birth control, ample evidence of just how far gone she was. Completely insane.

She still didn't care.

The sofa was big and wide, so there was plenty of room for them to lie side by side. Hank kissed her some more as he stroked and kneaded her breasts, pausing every now and then to kiss her nipples, teasing them to hard peaks with his clever tongue. The stimulation was almost too much for her. She made strange sounds in her throat as he stroked her belly and then the dark curls of her mound. Her entire concentration became focused on those few square inches of her body as, with each stroke, he grew bolder, inching closer to those once forbidden areas. Each time he dipped a finger to caress the soft folds between her legs, she gasped. And then he was gently probing, exploring, as tension built inside her. It felt as if she were breathing in gallons and gallons of air and forgetting to exhale.

All it took was one innocent brush against the ultrasensitive nub of her sex, and she exploded. Wave after wave of ecstasy poured over her, shimmering outward in golden ripples. She grabbed a pillow from the sofa and pressed it over her own face to stifle the screams, so his landlords wouldn't come running in the mistaken belief she was being killed.

Only she was dying, in a sense. *Petite morte,* that was what the French called a sexual climax. *Little death.* She'd learned that in some literature class, but it only now made sense.

Hank slid his hands underneath her shoulders and hugged her to him, grinning with obvious delight.

"Proud of yourself, are you?" she said when she could again form words. "That was a bit sudden. I would have waited for you, you know."

"Simultaneous climax is overrated. Maybe even a myth. I prefer going one at a time. That way I can enjoy yours, as well as mine."

She threw one leg over his, bringing his arousal into close contact with her. "Then let's move on to yours." She spoke the words boldly, but she was still a little apprehensive.

He kissed her, a sweet, soft kiss, then reached for the packet on the floor. In moments, he'd sheathed himself.

He coaxed her legs open, not rushing, ever patient. Perhaps he could sense her slight tension. But soon his languid strokes to her thighs and belly relaxed her. And when he moved atop her, she didn't even blink when he slid inside her, smooth as silk.

No pain. Not even slight discomfort. Just the exquisite sensation of fullness, of completion.

Then he began to move, and it wasn't complete at all.

It was just starting and it got even better. With each stroke, she felt him more deeply.

She opened her eyes, longing to see his face, to know what he was thinking and feeling. But the subtle expressions of his face remained a mystery to her. She could see that his eyes were closed, his brow slightly wrinkled, his mouth firm. She tried to put it all together, but she still couldn't figure it out.

So she focused on her own feelings. Pressure was building as it had before, and she wondered if it was possible for her to climax again.

She'd barely acknowledged the thought when Hank's strokes became faster, stronger, and she was gasping for breath herself, and all the sudden it did happen again, perhaps not as explosively as the first time but unmistakable anyway. Only this time he joined her, releasing one sharp cry as he released the tension that had built.

When it was all over, they lay together, still as death, for several minutes.

Finally, Willow found her voice. "What were you saying about simultaneous—"

"All right, all right, maybe I was mistaken."

"That was no myth. And I can't believe it's overrated."

He smiled and withdrew from her. She missed him already. She was already wondering when they could do this again. Oh, she was bad.

She adjusted her position slightly as Hank moved to lie beside her.

"So it was okay?" he asked.

"You don't need to fish for compliments. Of course it was okay. It was fantastic." She caressed his jaw and kissed him gently.

"Well, you can't blame me for being a little worried. I mean, after the last time…" His voice trailed off.

"The last time what?"

"You know. I was so stupid and clumsy back then. I might have been a little older than you, but I didn't have any more experience than you did, and you weren't ready. I know that now."

Willow tried to swallow, her mouth suddenly dry. He couldn't mean what it sounded like he meant. Was he…was he some guy from college who'd made an unsuccessful pass at her? Yes, that could be it. That had to be it.

His next words, though, were a cold dose of reality.

"I was afraid," he continued. "I just knew you'd go off to California and fall in love with some surfer boy and I'd never see you again. I wanted to be your first. I thought if you—if we made love, we'd be closer."

Willow felt a scream of panic building inside her. She tamped it down. How could it be? How could this man be Cal Chandler? She would recognize Cal, of all people. She knew his face as well as her own.

But there was the problem, right? She didn't know her own face.

"Willow, you're not saying anything."

She tried not to let the panic overtake her. She scrambled off the sofa, away from him, snatching up her clothes and fleeing to the bathroom without a word.

Chapter Four

"You idiot," Cal muttered as he searched for his own clothes. He couldn't leave well enough alone. He'd just *had* to bring up the past, to remind her of the single most devastating event in her life.

Still, he didn't understand the panic he'd seen in Willow's eyes as she'd bolted from his arms. It was as if he'd just reminded her of something she'd totally forgotten. But he knew she couldn't have forgotten. No woman could possibly forget losing her virginity in such spectacular fashion.

He gave her no more than a couple of minutes to collect herself. Then he walked down the hall to the bathroom and stood in front of the closed door. "Willow, are you okay?"

"Leave me alone."

"Okay, but I should warn you about what's in the bathtub."

Willow shrieked and the door flew open instantaneously. "Why are you keeping a snake in your bathtub?" she demanded.

"I ran over its tail in the driveway by accident. I couldn't just let it lie there and die."

She shook her head and flounced past him. She was fully dressed now, he noticed, except for her shoes.

He tucked his shirttails in and followed her. "I'm sorry I brought up the past. I thought maybe after all these years it wouldn't upset you anymore."

She stopped suddenly and whirled around, and he almost collided with him. "You think that's why I'm upset?"

"I don't know what else it would be." He really didn't.

"You and Nana cooked up this whole scheme, I bet. First you took the red flower out of your jacket so I wouldn't know it was you."

"What?"

"Then she made sure she was gone when I came out to meet you so I'd still be in the dark. You thought if I had my defenses down I'd...I'd do just exactly what I did. Oh, my God!"

Cal wasn't following any of this. "Willow, please—"

"Don't you 'Willow, please' me." She turned again, marched into the living room, and found her shoes and her purse.

"Just tell me why you're mad."

She shoved her feet into the sandals, not bothering to buckle them. "You don't think I have a right to be mad when I just had sex with someone I've been thinking of as 'Hank' all night long?"

"What?" he said yet again. This was either the worst nightmare of his life, or he'd dropped into *The Twilight Zone.*

"Yeah, Hank. You never talked about the past, so I had no hope of catching on. You even disguised your voice."

"What's my voice got to do with anything? I spent a

week with tubes down my throat. My vocal cords were damaged."

That stopped her.

"Willow, are you trying to tell me you didn't know who I was?"

She closed her eyes, as if in pain. "Just take me home, please."

"Not until you answer my question." It didn't seem possible that she wouldn't know him. Granted, they hadn't seen much of each other over the past five years, but he hadn't changed much. He'd grown an inch or two, filled out some, but she'd had no trouble recognizing him last year when they'd run into each other at the Chatsworths' fish fry.

Then something awful occurred to him. "Is something wrong with your vision? Your accident—"

"I can see fine."

"Then what?"

"You honestly don't know? Nana didn't tell you?"

"She didn't tell me anything."

"If you take me home, I'll tell you on the way."

OUTWARDLY, WILLOW had calmed down a bit by the time she climbed into Cal's truck. Inwardly she still trembled with disbelief and outrage.

She'd made love with Cal, her enemy for life, the person who would be at the very bottom of her list of men she wanted to have sex with.

And she'd loved every minute of it. That was the weird part.

So she told him about her head injury. And she told him again, when he didn't quite get it the first time.

"You're telling me you really didn't have any idea I was me?" he asked for the third time.

"No idea."

"But how could you—"

"I don't know. You dropped enough clues. All the animals, the fact you work at the Hardison Ranch, your fondness for Nana's cookies. But I'd ruled you out. See, at the wedding you wore that red flower in your buttonhole all night. And the man I'd danced with didn't have a flower."

"Sherry Hardison took it, right before I asked you to dance."

Well, that explained that, she supposed. "How come you never talked about the past?" she wanted to know. "Not a single trip down memory lane the whole night."

"I didn't want to bring up any painful memories. I wanted to focus on the future. I thought you'd finally forgiven me and we were having a fresh start."

She had nothing to say to that. She wanted to forgive him. She wanted to be the kind of person who could forgive past transgressions. But she couldn't get past what had happened five years ago. Even now, she was still suffering from the repercussions of that hot summer evening when, thinking they would have the house to themselves for hours, they'd done what they'd been talking about doing for months.

Before "the incident," she'd been slated to attend Stanford University, and her parents were going to foot the whole bill. But that offer had been jerked away. Five years ago, they'd told her that a girl who could throw all her parents' wise counsel and advice out the window and betray their trust in their own home could damn well work her way through college. They'd never wavered an inch from their earlier decision.

It had taken her five years to work her way through college—first junior college, then a state university. Because she'd been working three jobs, her grades had not been the best. She'd had to give up visions of Harvard Medical School. A dozen less prestigious schools had rejected her. It was a minor miracle she'd been accepted at UT Southwestern.

Her relationship with her parents was still strained.

"Well, I can't change the past," Cal said with a fatalistic sigh. "If it's not in you to forgive, or to at least try to understand my side of things, then we have nothing left to talk about."

Willow realized he'd pulled up in front of Nana's house. A few minutes earlier, she'd been so eager to escape Cal she would have clawed her way out through the wall of his apartment. Now she felt an odd reluctance to leave.

"Thank you for dinner and the cruise and…" Her face burned. "Well, for everything."

He made a disgusted noise in the back of his throat, and he wouldn't look at her. "Maybe you better just go."

She did. She felt she should have said something else. It didn't feel right now, just walking away. Maybe she should have listened to what he had to say in his own defense.

But then she hardened her heart. He had no idea the hell she'd gone through to get to the brink of a medical career. How could she possibly forgive him?

She heard his old truck chug away as she stuck her key in the front-door lock.

WILLOW HARDLY SLEPT at all. She lay on her girlish twin bed and relived every moment—all that she could remember, anyway—of what would have been the best date of her life, if she could just lop off the last few minutes. She managed to finally drift off, then ended up sleeping late into the morning.

When she awoke at almost ten, she immediately felt a heavy sense of dread settle around her heart. She didn't want to confront Nana, who'd already been in bed asleep when Willow had arrived home from her date.

Really, how could her grandmother *do* something like that to her? Sending her off, blissfully ignorant, on a date with Cal Chandler. It was unconscionable. Willow loved her grandmother, and she knew Nana had good intentions. But she'd completely crossed the line this time. Willow needed to let Nana know the consequences of her meddling.

However, the house was quiet and the kitchen dark when Willow came downstairs. There was a note on the refrigerator: *Had some errands to run.* Errands, right. Nana was avoiding Willow. *P.S. Don't forget lunch at Miracle Café.*

With a gasp, Willow grabbed the notebook she kept on a cord around her neck. She wrote down *everything* and consulted it frequently—it was the only way she could function with her short-circuited memory. She flipped frantically through the pages. Oh, shoot, there it was. Lunch with Mom and Dad, noon Monday, Miracle Café.

Willow groaned. Though her parents both had hovered near her bedside when she was in critical condition after the accident, she hadn't seen them at all since coming home from the hospital. They'd all agreed that since they both worked full-time, Willow should recuperate at Nana's. It hadn't occurred to either one of them to take off a few days from work to take care of their daughter who'd almost died.

They just weren't the nurturing, warm-and-fuzzy type. Willow had long ago realized and accepted that. But they'd given her many other things for which she was grateful, she reminded herself. She'd inherited a keen intellect from both of them. They both had advanced degrees from prestigious institutions. She'd also learned her work ethic from them. Idle hands hadn't been allowed in her parents' house. They'd encouraged her to be the best she could and not to settle for mediocrity.

Unfortunately, along with the encouragement came a lot of criticism. They'd been especially tough on her ever since "the incident." It was as if they'd completely lost their trust in her and now *expected* her to make stupid decisions.

She could just imagine what they would say if they knew about her date with Cal. But Nana wouldn't breathe a word. Her grandmother was the soul of discretion and far more open-minded than Willow's parents.

Willow dressed carefully in a very conservative outfit, navy slacks with a short-sleeved, pinstripe blouse. She pulled her hair into a bun and made sure that no tendrils of hair escaped. She applied only a small amount of makeup. No sense giving them anything to criticize right off the bat.

She purposely arrived early at the Miracle Café and ordered some sweet tea to sip on. That way she didn't have to search among the tables to find anyone, which would be an impossible task.

To her surprise, Nana showed up before Willow's parents.

"Nana, I didn't know you were coming."

"I thought you could use some moral support, in case they start—Well, you know how they can be sometimes."

Oh, yeah. Willow was grateful for Nana's presence. But then she remembered she was still mad.

"So, aren't you going to ask me about my date?"

"Er, I figured you'd tell me about it when you were ready." Nana fidgeted with her napkin. "You got in late. You must have had a good time," she added with false brightness.

Willow folded her arms. "Nana, how could you do that to me? How could you send me out on a date with Cal Chandler when you know how I feel about him?"

Nana gazed at her for a few silent seconds. Then she looked down into her lap. "I have no possible way to defend myself. It was a craven and cowardly act, not to mention meddlesome, for me to fake a bingo game." She grabbed her water and gulped from it.

"You're not getting away with this. I know all your tricks. When you don't want to argue, you just agree with me and take all my good lines."

"All right. If you want an argument, I'll give you one. I did what I did precisely because I know how you feel about Cal. You still love him."

Willow looked around worriedly to see if anyone had heard. But no one was seated near them. "I hate him," she whispered. Even as she said it, she knew it wasn't true.

"There's a fine line between love and hate," Nana

said. She paused long enough to order some tea, then waited until the waitress had left. "If you really had no lingering feelings for him, you wouldn't feel strongly one way or another. You'd be indifferent. You'd have fallen in love three or four more times by now. I thought if you could just spend some time with him, you'd remember how happy he once made you and you'd get off your high horse."

Willow shredded the paper from her straw, too agitated to keep her hands still. "Well, it worked out exactly as you wanted, then."

Nana looked hopeful. "It did?"

"I had a great time. We dined, we danced, we gazed at the stars. And I was thinking, 'Where has this wonderful man been all my life?' And all the while, I was calling him Hank in my mind because I didn't know his name."

"When did you figure it out? Surely after a few minutes of conversation—"

"Nope. Didn't catch on. Didn't have a clue. Not even when I went to his place and saw that he kept his own private zoo. Not even when he kissed me. No spark of familiarity at all."

Nana's eyes got wider and wider. "Then when—"

Willow lowered her voice again. "Not until *after* we made love."

Nana choked on her water.

"Yup, that's right. I had sex with a man whose name I didn't know."

"But you did know him. That's my point. Deep down, some part of you knew he was the man you loved. Otherwise, you never would have— I mean, that's not like you at all."

With that, all the fight went out of Willow. She sipped her tea and looked out the plate glass window onto the square. Everywhere, normal people were going about their normal business as if the world hadn't fallen off its axis last night.

Nana took her hand. "I'm sorry, sweetheart. I'm so sorry this all went awry. I never in a million years thought it would go as far as it did."

"Did you know it was him, even at the wedding?" Willow had to ask.

"No, dear. I truly didn't know it was him until he showed up at the door. Then I just couldn't make myself go up to your bedroom and tell you because I knew you wouldn't go out with him. You wouldn't have even come out of your room."

That was true enough, Willow conceded.

"I thought Cal deserved a chance. He's a good man. I never told you this, but he still visits me when he can. He mows my grass and does fix-it projects for me."

"He does?"

"And he's never tried to use my fondness for him to get to you. He does things for me out of kindness. Men like that don't grow on trees, you know."

Willow dabbed at her eyes with her napkin. It wouldn't do to cry, not when her parents would be there any minute. They would want to know why she was upset, and what could she possibly tell them?

"He's not the man for me, Nana. Even if I could get past what happened. He has no ambition, no goals, no plans in life. He's just floating along, underutilizing his brain, a big kid who doesn't want to grow up."

"All right, Willow. We won't talk about it again."

She studied the menu as if she didn't know it by heart. "What are you going to get for lunch?"

"I don't even have time to deal with men," Willow continued despite her grandmother's attempt to close the conversation. "I can't imagine what I was thinking when I agreed to go out on a date, anyway. Only five weeks until medical school, and my brain is still as scrambled as ever."

"Whatever you say, dear."

"You're doing it again."

"What?"

"Agreeing with me."

"Because you're making perfect sense. Cal is lazy and immature, all he's interested in is sex and you don't have time for men anyway. What's to argue with?"

"I never said all he was interested in was sex."

"Well, he must have pressured you. Why else would you do that on a first date?"

"If anything, I pressured him," she admitted. "He tried to talk me out of it."

"Willow Marsden!"

"Yeah, I know."

They didn't talk any further about Cal because Dave and Marianne Marsden arrived. Though Willow didn't immediately recognize their faces, they were the only successful, conservative bankers with matching navy suits in the place.

Willow greeted them with dutiful hugs. Then her parents settled into their chairs.

Dave immediately flagged the waitress. "We already know what we want," he said, never one to dillydally.

"We can't stay too long," Marianne said apologetically. "Minor crisis at work."

There was always a minor crisis at work, but Willow didn't mention that.

They made small talk until the food arrived. Dave cut small, neat bites from his broiled chicken breast, while Marianne nibbled daintily at a chef salad. Nana dug into a perfectly cooked chicken-fried steak, while Willow was trying to enjoy a hickory-smoked hamburger.

It was hard to appreciate the grilled burger, though, when she was about to get her own grilling.

"So, how's the outpatient therapy going?" Dave asked. "You're going, aren't you?"

"Yes, Dad. Every day."

"Are you seeing any progress?" Marianne asked anxiously.

"No." That wasn't a hundred percent true. She had shown some slight improvement in her memory. Nana said she wasn't repeating herself as much—which she did because she sometimes couldn't remember a conversation she'd had ten minutes earlier. And she managed to remember all the salient details of her date with Cal, the one thing she wished she could forget.

"Well, I don't see how you can go to medical school in your condition," Dave observed. "You'll have to put it off a year."

"I can't do that," Willow explained patiently. "I would have to reapply, and they probably wouldn't take me again." It wasn't as if medical schools across the country were competing to get her.

"If you hadn't gotten into that car with Mick Dewhurst in the first place—"

"Dad, don't start," Willow pleaded. "Can't we just have a nice lunch? Does everything have to be focused on me?"

"You're the one whose life is in a state of flux," Dave said. "We have to get you straightened out. Anyway, you *like* for things to focus on you."

"That's not true," she said in a bewildered voice, wondering why her father would say something like that. "And I *am* straightened out. I'm working on my memory. I do exercises every day. I've still got more than a month before school."

"Maybe you need to take your mind off it," Marianne said. "You could come work at the bank!"

Dave gave his wife a look that said she'd just come up with the stupidest idea ever. "She can't work at the bank. What if she couldn't tell the difference between Washington and Lincoln?"

"Oh, I guess you're right. And if she couldn't recognize our customers, they might be insulted."

"She couldn't anyway," Nana said. "She's starting her temporary job this weekend."

Willow froze. Job? What job? How could she have forgotten something as important as a job? She discreetly checked her notebook, which she'd tucked into her purse. Oh, shoot, there it was. She'd agreed to work as a cook at Wade Hardison's rodeo camp for a couple of weeks while his regular cook took a vacation. She did have a job.

Dave snorted. "I don't know why you would waste your time doing something so beneath your abilities."

She didn't bother to explain that simple tasks were all she could handle right now. She'd been working part-time over the summer as an emergency dispatcher, but she certainly didn't trust herself to continue *that* work in her current condition. She would be putting people's lives at risk if her memory failed her at a crucial moment.

"I think working at the camp will be good for you, dear," Nana put in. "You'll get some fresh air, work with children—that's something you enjoy. And it'll take your mind off your problems. Nothing makes your problems seem small like helping other people with *their* problems."

Dave snorted again. "I'd hardly call Willow's problems small."

Willow wasn't really looking forward to working at the camp. It had seemed like a good idea when Nana had arranged it for her. She could cook; at least, she could handle the simple fare she imagined might be required at summer camp. And she did like kids. She had first-aid training which might come in handy at a summer camp.

But there was just one problem. Wade Hardison's camp and horse-breeding operation were right down the road from his older brother's ranch. And that was a little too close to Cal Chandler for comfort.

"So," Marianne said, briskly changing the subject. "My friend Winona Wilson said she saw you last night on the Party Barge."

Willow's stomach suddenly felt queasy. "I hope she didn't think I was rude if I didn't say hi to her."

"Oh, no, you were apparently way across the dance floor. And dancing with a very handsome man, Winona said."

Uh-oh, here it comes.

"So, who was it?" Dave didn't mince words.

"Yes, I'll admit I'm curious," Marianne added. "I didn't know you were dating anyone."

"I'm not," Willow said hastily. "He was just some-one I ran into at Mick's and Tonya's wedding."

Please don't ask. Please don't ask.

"Who?" Dave and Marianne said together.

Willow sighed. If she'd been able to come up with the name of some suitable bachelor her parents wouldn't object to, she would have told a boldfaced lie. But her faulty memory wouldn't cooperate.

She looked to Nana for help.

"It was that nice Cal Chandler," Nana said.

Suddenly, it felt as if the second Ice Age had just vis-ited the Miracle Café. Both Dave's and Marianne's forks froze in midair.

"Well," her mother finally said. As if that summed it up.

"I know what you're thinking," Willow jumped in, forestalling the torrent of objections she knew was com-ing. "I thought he was someone else when I accepted the date. You know, because of the face-blind thing." Her parents never had really understood her condition. "Then I just couldn't back out gracefully. But don't worry, I won't be seeing him again."

Dave wiped his mouth with his napkin. "I should hope not."

Nana dropped her fork into her plate. It rattled loudly, causing several other people in the restaurant to look over. "Oh, would you two get over it!"

"Get *over* it?" Marianne repeated. "Are we supposed to forget the fact that Cal Chandler—"

"Just stop right there," Willow said. "We are not dis-cussing this, not again. Nana is right. It's ancient his-tory, and we all need to forget it and move on."

"Anyway," Nana said tightly, "I should think you

owe Cal your gratitude. He gave you the perfect excuse to keep your precious Willow home with you."

Dave's face paled. "Excuse me, Mother?"

"You couldn't stand the fact that she was flying from the nest. You'd spent the last eighteen years doting on your only child, controlling every aspect of her existence, and you couldn't face life without her. So you used her youthful indiscretion as an excuse to keep her under your thumb a little longer."

Willow stared first at her grandmother, then at her parents, not quite believing what she'd just heard. She'd never seen Nana take her gloves off like this before.

Dave threw his napkin onto the table. "That is the most ridiculous—" But he stopped when Marianne squeezed his arm.

"You know, Clea," Marianne said quietly, "there might be just the tiniest bit of truth in what you just said." She looked at Willow. "We do love you so much. Maybe too much. It was hard for us, imagining you all the way out in California with no one to turn to if you got into trouble.…"

"So you did the one thing that was sure to turn Willow against you," Clea said.

"In retrospect, it doesn't seem as if we handled things very well," Dave grumbled. He put his napkin back in his lap and resumed eating.

The table went silent for the next few minutes. Willow couldn't eat any more of her burger, so she sipped her tea. Was it possible her grandmother was right? Had her parents flipped out and forbade her to go to Stanford partly because they would have been lonely without her?

Chapter Five

"This is the best breakfast I ever ate."

That enthusiastic proclamation had come from a thin African-American boy with a scar by his left ear. Sitting on a camp stool by the small morning fire enjoying her own breakfast, Willow quickly shuffled through files in her mental computer, struggling to identify the speaker by his jumble of physical features.

After a moment she smiled. Damon, that was his name. More often than not, her mental computer tossed out some irrelevant piece of information when she asked it nicely for a name.

But some, like Damon, she remembered more easily than others. The ten-year-old had been caught breaking into his neighbor's house to steal anything that could be pawned. He'd spent the first week of camp bragging about his various exploits. Now that they were into the second week, he spent more time talking about his horse, Danny, than the street gangs back home.

Though Willow had been apprehensive about working as a cook at the Hardison Rodeo Camp, she was glad now she was here. It was amazing to watch the transformations taking place in these kids, some of whom had never seen a horse before. And, as Nana had pointed out, seeing and hearing about the problems these children faced—and sometimes that meant just getting enough to eat—made her feel better about her own situation.

In fact, sometimes she felt downright small and petty for fretting so much about her cognitive difficulties, annoying as those might be.

She had seen no sign of Cal, thank goodness, though he worked just down the road. She wanted to talk to him at some point, but not until she'd straightened out in her mind whether she could stop blaming him for the disastrous events of that long-ago summer.

"Can I have seconds?" Damon asked.

"Please," Willow added, then smiled. "Yes, of course you may have seconds."

The breakfast Damon was so happy about was the same one they'd eaten almost every morning—biscuit dough stuck on the end of a stick and cooked over the open fire. When it was done, you pulled it off the stick and filled it with jelly and butter. It was something Willow had learned in Girl Scouts. She also fixed the campers scrambled eggs and bacon.

One by one, the kids finished and brought their plates to the picnic table, scraping them into the trash and stacking them neatly. Anyone who didn't follow the procedure might get stuck washing dishes, so they'd learned the routine pretty quickly.

They drifted off to the corral, where horses of various sizes milled around, awaiting their temporary masters. Wade was going to let a couple of the older boys—and one determined girl—try bull riding. The bull was gentle as a lamb and the kids would be well padded, but they were excited.

Two college-aged counselors would work with the younger kids on their roping skills.

Willow hummed to herself as she banked the campfire. Now that she knew her own routine, she found the tasks pleasant and undemanding. Her thoughts drifted, as they often did, to her evening with Cal and her conflicted feelings about it.

Once Nana had convinced her that Cal really hadn't known of her disability, her anger toward him had cooled considerably. He'd been as much a victim of circumstances as she. He hadn't brought up the past, but neither had she. She'd done her level best to conceal her cognitive problems from him. If she'd just admitted she didn't know who he was from the very beginning, the whole thing never would have happened. So she was as much to blame as anyone.

But it had happened. And while her unreliable memory managed to conceal from her important things like the date of her next doctor's appointment or what she'd just read in the morning paper, it supplied her with the memory of every moment of her date with Cal with unerring accuracy.

She wished for the hundredth time that the man she'd been so ga-ga over that night could be anyone but Cal.

Suddenly a horse's panicked whinny grabbed her attention, followed by a child's cry of panic. She dropped everything and ran for the practice ring, along with everyone else within hearing distance.

As soon as she got there, she saw the problem. A child lay on his back on the dirt, struggling to breathe.

And a riderless horse stood a few feet away, the reins of his bridle dragging in the dirt.

Wade arrived just as she did. "What happened?"

Several kids tried to talk at once, but Tara, one of the counselors, shushed them. "Danny threw him," she said, obviously distressed. "Damon was just about to start a warm-up walk around the ring. I didn't see anything that would cause the horse to panic like that."

"Danny?" Wade repeated, clearly shocked.

Willow was already on her knees beside Damon. He was conscious but struggling for breath.

"He may have just gotten the wind knocked out of him," Willow said, hoping that was the case. "Damon, does anything hurt?"

"No," he croaked, trying to get up. Willow held his shoulder down. "Don't move just yet. Can you wiggle your feet? How about your fingers?"

Damon did as asked. After a cursory examination, Willow determined that he wasn't seriously injured. Nothing but his pride, anyway. So she let him sit up slowly.

"Wade, why'd Danny throw me?" Damon asked, almost in tears. "I been nothing but nice to that horse. I didn't hit him or yank on the reins or nothing."

Wade came down on one knee and put his arm around Damon's thin shoulders. "There are only two reasons a horse acts like that. Something hurt him, or something scared him. Think you can stand?"

"Yeah, I'm okay."

Wade helped the boy to his feet, then led him back to the now placid horse. "Take his reins. We'll lead him back to the barn and take off his tack. Could be he has a burr under his saddle."

Damon was apprehensive at first, but he soon real-ized the horse meant him no harm and he led him away.

By lunch time, Damon had become something of a hero—the only camper to be thrown from a horse this session—and he was making the most of the incident, elaborating more with each telling.

But as Willow assembled turkey sandwiches at the end of the table under the shaded pavilion, her attention was more on what the adults were saying. Wade was re-counting his own version of the story to his wife, Anne, who joined the campers for lunch a couple of days a week, when she could get away from her law office.

"I checked that horse from nose to tail, didn't see anything physically wrong with him," Wade said. "Tara says no one was near him except Damon, and all Damon did was nudge him with his heels. This is the first time Danny's ever thrown anybody."

"What are you going to do?" Anne asked as she fed a morsel of cheese to her one-year-old daughter, Olivia.

"I can't let the campers ride him anymore."

"Oh, no!" Willow said, almost without thinking. Both Wade and Anne looked at her, surprised.

"Sorry, I couldn't help overhearing. Danny *loves* working with the kids. You can't retire him."

"I can't endanger the kids, either. He's an old horse—over twenty, I think. Sometimes the minds of old horses start to go. They get senile, just like people."

"You should call Cal," Anne said. "Remember how he worked out that problem with Cimmaron last year?"

Cimmaron was the horse Wade had claimed a na-tional calf-roping championship with two years ago. "What problem did she have?" Willow asked, realizing as she did that she was hungry for any story that had to do with Cal.

"She used to shy at just about anything," Wade answered. "Someone twenty feet away could pull out a handkerchief, and she'd go into orbit. Cal cured her of that."

"He does have an uncanny way with horses," Anne agreed. "He works with all our foals now. He gentles them down in no time, almost like magic." Then a shadow crossed Anne's face. "You used to date him, didn't you?"

How refreshing. Someone who didn't know the story. Well, Anne had been away at college and Wade had been following the rodeo circuit when her spectacular breakup with Cal had caused all the town gossips' tongues to wag.

"A long time ago," Willow answered, trying to sound nonchalant.

"You won't mind if we bring him out here, will you?"

"Oh, of course not," Willow replied a bit too quickly. "You just go right ahead. Do whatever you have to do to help Danny." And she would hide in the kitchen.

OF COURSE, SHE didn't hide in the kitchen. Like everyone else at the camp, she went to watch Cal with Danny. She was starving for the sight of him—even if she wouldn't really recognize him when she saw him.

She stepped up on the bottom rail of the corral fence and pulled herself up so she could see. Flanked on either side by a line of campers who were as curious as she was, she hoped she could blend into the crowd so that Cal wouldn't even notice her.

And for a while, he didn't. His attention was focused so totally on Danny, the fat old plug, that someone could have set a bomb off in the ring and he wouldn't have noticed.

She wasn't sure what she expected him to do, but his behavior certainly surprised her. He spent at least ten minutes standing in front of the horse, his face close to Danny's long nose, staring into the beast's eyes and rhythmically stroking its jaw.

She thought his lips were moving, too, though if he was actually saying something, she couldn't hear the words.

But she could imagine them. He would speak in soft, soothing tones until the horse relaxed. The words wouldn't matter. Just the attitude his voice communicated would relax the animal, make it receptive to—

Willow shook herself. She was the one Cal talked into being receptive. But he wasn't talking to her—he was talking to the horse. Who cared what he said to a horse?

Cal pursed his lips. Was he blowing into the horse's nose? The horse dipped his head down to the ground, almost as if he were bowing to Cal. Cal grinned and scratched behind both ears.

He looked up then, as if only now aware of the crowd of people watching him. He smiled, almost as if he were embarrassed to be caught having this intimate conversation with an animal.

Then his gaze caught hers. He froze for about half a second, then abruptly turned his attention back to the horse.

Well, she couldn't blame him. They hadn't parted on very good terms. He probably thought she was a complete lunatic, now that he'd had time to ponder her behavior that night, and wanted nothing to do with her.

SPOTTING WILLOW'S face in the crowd had momentarily thrown Cal off his rhythm. What the hell was she doing here? Had he hallucinated her, just because he'd been thinking about her night and day for the last two weeks?

He would deal with Willow later. He couldn't afford to let his concentration waver. Danny was depending on him. He would never admit this aloud, but he would almost swear the horse knew what was going on. He knew he was in some kind of trouble, and he sensed Cal was there to help him.

Cal took the horse's ears and squeezed the tips, then worked his fingers back toward the head, then along the back of the neck where the mane grew out. The horse nickered softly, obviously liking the gentle massage.

Cal took his time, moved on past the withers and along the back, the rump, to the tail. Danny stood stock still, head down, nose almost touching the ground.

"Atta boy, Danny," Cal murmured.

He knew this horse. He remembered when Jonathan's son used to ride Danny before he'd graduated to a more spirited mount. A gentler, sweeter-tempered animal didn't exist. If Danny had bucked someone off, there was a serious problem.

With the horse in a receptive, almost trance-like state, Cal examined him from head to toe, starting with the teeth and gums and working backward, feeling along every square inch of his sleek brown hair. He'd watched his father and grandfather do this enough times to know the routine, but he wasn't looking for precisely the same things as a vet would. Cal's examination was a bit more…esoteric.

He kept an eye on Danny's head, and particularly his ears, as he moved his hands to different parts of the horse's body. He listened for the swish of his tail or the scuff of a hoof in the sand. Any small movement might indicate he'd found a sensitive area. He felt for a tell-tale quiver of muscles, a change in tension that might indicate an elevation in stress.

He was beginning to think he would find nothing. Who was he kidding? He wasn't some magician who could magically cure—

And then he felt something at a spot just inside Danny's left rear leg. There was nothing on the skin, no lumps under the flesh to indicate disease or injury. But when Cal rubbed that area, the horse shifted his weight, just slightly. Probably no one watching could see it, but Cal felt it.

He pressed a bit harder, and Danny's left rear hoof lifted just slightly, as if he wanted to kick Cal's hand away but was too well-mannered.

That was it, then. Danny was in pain. Probably when the little boy had kicked him to urge him forward, he'd somehow aggravated the condition, whatever it was, and panicked the horse.

He wasn't sure what his audience expected, but they were probably going to be disappointed. He motioned for Wade to come over, then showed him the area in question.

Wade bent down to have a look. "I don't see anything."

"You can't see it. You can't feel it, either. But he can."

"How do you know?"

Cal shrugged. "I just do."

"Does he have a tumor or something?"

"You'll have to ask my grandfather to figure out the pathology. I'm not a vet. I just know that's where he's hurting. If you take him to Granddad's office, he's got all kinds of fancy diagnostic tools."

Wade straightened, smiled, and shook his head. "We'll see."

Then Cal realized he had a shadow, a little African-American boy who was standing silently at his elbow. "Hey," Cal greeted the boy. "Are you the one Danny tossed?"

The boy nodded. "Is he okay?"

"He's got a sore spot. You probably kicked it by accident. There's no way you could have known, so don't feel bad."

The boy stood up straighter. "He's the one should feel bad. He broke the rules, not me." But then he grinned. "Miss Willow gave me a carrot. Can I give it to him?"

Miss Willow, huh? "Sure."

Cal watched for a few moments as the boy and the horse cemented their friendship. Then he went to find "Miss Willow." Apparently he hadn't been hallucinating. Was she here in some official capacity?

She'd disappeared from the fence where he'd last seen her, and as the campers and counselors returned to their normal activities, he didn't spot her.

"Looking for someone?" Wade asked.

"Willow Marsden. Is she working here or something?"

"She's filling in for Sally, our cook. She probably went back up to the house." Wade gave him a knowing smile before returning to his own duties.

Aw, hell. Cal wondered what Willow had told her employers about him. Over the past few years she hadn't had many kind words to say about him. But if she'd bad-mouthed him to the Hardisons—

He nixed that thought. Willow harbored a lot of pain and anger, but she wasn't publicly vindictive.

It might be crazy for him to go in search of her after their disastrous date, but he wasn't going to get this close to her and not try to talk to her. He at least wanted to know why she was working here.

And he wanted to find out how her recovery was coming along. Nana had told him, confidentially, that Willow's doctors were hopeful her cognitive impairment was only temporary. Hopeful, but not optimistic. If she'd been a child whose brain was still developing, the damage might repair itself. But she was an adult, albeit a young one, so the outcome wasn't certain.

He'd been wondering what that meant in terms of medical school. Now he would ask her himself—if she would talk to him.

He found her in the kitchen of the huge old farmhouse, kneading a slab of dough. The way she was digging her fingers into the dough, then balling it up and whamming it against the floured butcher-block counter, made him glad he wasn't the dough.

"Willow?"

She jumped. "Oh, I didn't see you there," she said politely, flashing an embarrassed smile.

"Obviously. You were busy giving that dough a piece of your mind." He took off his hat and stepped closer.

"It's very therapeutic, kneading dough. And those campers have a never-ending appetite for breads of all kinds, so I have plenty of opportunity."

He came closer. "What exactly do you need therapy for?"

She froze and looked up, studying him intently. Then she looked at his dog, sitting obediently by the door. "Oh, hell, it's you."

"You mean you *still* don't recognize—"

"Shh. Keep it down. Not everyone around here realizes my little problem. No, I didn't recognize you. I thought you were Wade—cowboy hat, tight jeans, boots. If I'd been paying closer attention, I probably could have figured it out by your voice. But I wasn't expecting you in here."

"And you were distracted," Cal added, still amazed that he could stand a few feet from her and she wouldn't know him. At least she was talking to him.

She resumed her kneading, more gently now. "Why are you here?"

"Why do you think?"

"Because you just can't get enough of me saying *no*?" But she softened the comment by adding, "You were pretty amazing out there. I think that horse would have crawled into your lap if you'd have let him. Did you solve the problem?"

Cal shrugged. "Possibly."

"Danny's not going senile, is he?"

"No. He's got a tumor or an infection or something that gave him a sore spot. Granddad will have to diagnose it and treat it."

"How could you figure that out by what you did?"

Again, he shrugged. People had been asking him all his life how he got animals to do what he wanted them to do. It seemed simple to him, though not so simple to explain. "I read his body language."

"And what was that business with breathing into his nose?"

"Horses like that. They learn a lot more through their sense of smell than we do. It's a way to bond with them."

Willow reached for a rolling pin hanging from an overhead rack and began rolling out the dough. "Why did you drop out of vet school?" she asked abruptly.

The question took him by surprise. A lot of people had wanted to know the answer three years ago when he'd withdrawn from Texas A&M's veterinary medicine program, and he hadn't provided a good answer then.

He still wasn't completely sure. "I'm not cut out to be a vet."

"In what way?"

"Is it important that you know?" he countered.

Willow pulled a biscuit cutter from a drawer and began cutting precise discs out of the dough, pressing and twisting on the utensil with more force than he thought necessary. "I guess you're right. Your reasons for trashing your life aren't any of my concern."

"Trashing my— Is that what you think I did?"

"You had every advantage in the world," she said through gritted teeth, "starting with a brilliant mind and the ability to apply it. You had parents and an extended family who supported you every step of the way, who never questioned anything, even when you took chances or made choices they didn't approve of. You had plenty of money—your parents paid for everything. You never had to work and go to school at the same time. You got accepted to every vet school you applied to, first try— almost unheard of. And then you just threw it all away and became a *ranch hand*."

"When we were on the Party Barge, you thought being a ranch hand was fine."

"That was before I knew you were you. It's good, honest work for someone whose choices are limited, or for people who are born into the lifestyle and have it in their blood. You don't fit into either of those categories."

She had him there.

"It's so clear to *anyone* who watched you out there today that you have a gift with animals. Why on earth wouldn't you put it to use by doing what you were meant to do?"

"Who says I was meant to do it? It was always assumed I would go to vet school because my father and grandfather were vets. But, unlike you, I didn't know from the time I could crawl what I wanted to be when I grew up."

"And I guess you still don't know?"

"I guess." He was on shakier ground now. Yeah, a twenty-six-year-old man should be doing something with his life. "Why the interrogation, Willow? I can think of lots more important things we should talk about."

"Like what?"

"Like why we aren't together."

"I can explain that. You ruined my life." She said it as if by rote.

"*I* ruined your life. In case you've forgotten, there were two of us under that blanket when your parents walked in on us."

"And only one of us wanted to be there."

"If you didn't want to make love with me, you should have said no."

"I said no. Not that night, maybe, but plenty of other nights. And you kept trying."

"That's what twenty-one-year-old males do."

She picked up what was left of the dough after she'd cut out two dozen biscuits and wadded it into a ball. She was ignoring Cal as much as she could.

"I'm sorry if I pressured you," he tried again. "But I'd waited three years, and you were eighteen. In another month, you were going off to college. I thought, if we didn't make love, I'd lose you. You'd fall in love with some blond beach bum, and he'd be your first, and I'd never see you again."

"And I thought if we didn't make love, you'd get tired of waiting and move on." Her voice was soft, sad. She still wouldn't look at him, just kept kneading the dough.

"I wouldn't have, though."

"I was too scared to test you any further."

That blew him away. He'd known she was scared—he was, too. Everybody was scared their first time. "You really didn't want sex?"

Finally, she looked at him. "I was a late bloomer. I mean a *real* late bloomer."

Chapter Six

Willow continued to knead her dough—these were going to be the tastiest biscuits on Earth. She waited for Cal to grasp the significance of what she'd just said.

Finally he did. "You mean you were...you hadn't..."

She nodded, embarrassed that she'd ever brought this up. But she supposed he needed to know. "I hit puberty a few months later." And she'd slowly begun to understand a lot of things as her body had awakened. But she hadn't fully appreciated what it meant to crave someone of the opposite sex until a week ago, when she and Cal had made love with such complete abandon. "As close as we were, I never felt like I could talk to you about that."

"I'm glad you told me," he said. Then he added, "You'd sure started looking like a woman."

"Let's not go there." She rolled the remaining dough out and cut some more biscuits.

"I'm sorry you think I ruined your life," Cal said. "But, you know, your life doesn't look so ruined to me. You're off to med school in, what, three weeks?"

"Maybe. Maybe not. Of course, that's not your fault."

"Seriously? You might not go?" He sounded so crushed, she wanted to throw her arms around him. But Cal was probably one of the few people who had been privy to her youthful dreams of becoming a doctor. She'd had a lot of ideas when she was younger—working for the Peace Corps, finding a cure for some terrible disease. She'd been idealistic, perhaps, but very passionate.

Cal remembered that, and it touched her.

"You've been blessed with an astounding memory," she said. "I've always had a good one, too, though not in your league. Now, imagine if your memory didn't work right anymore."

"But it's just faces you get confused with, right? I mean, how serious…"

"It's more than just faces." She arranged the last few biscuits onto the baking sheet. "Take these biscuits. I've been baking them every day for more than a week. But I have to read Anne's recipe every time. I can't remember how long to bake them or at what temperature. And see this?" She yanked on a small, spiral-bound notebook that hung from her neck on a piece of yarn, a strange-looking necklace. "I have to write down every single thing I'm supposed to do in this notebook and look at it fifty times a day, or I'll forget something."

"But you'll get better."

"Perhaps. Eventually."

"Then you'll put off med school for a year. It's not the end of the world."

She shook her head. "Not that easy. I would have to take the MCAT again, since it's been more than three years. Then, assuming by some miracle I do well on the test, I could reapply to med school. But realistically, they won't give me another shot, not if I suddenly withdraw for this year. They'll want to know why. And when I explain it…no medical school wants a brain-damaged student."

She slammed the oven door in frustration. "Sometimes there's a narrow window of opportunity. For me, this is it. It's now or never."

Cal's face sagged with disappointment. Or something. She still wasn't much good at deciphering expressions. "I don't know what to say. You've wanted this so much, and for so long—"

"You don't have to remind me."

"What will you do?"

"Get a job, I guess."

"Here in Cottonwood?"

"Oh, no. In Dallas or Houston, probably. I don't think I could stand living where everybody would know I was a failure." *Look, there goes that poor Willow. Brain-damaged, you know. Probably drools on herself. Had a promising future as a doctor until—*

"No one would think that. Give the people in this town some credit. I dropped out of vet school, but no one calls me a failure. Well, except maybe you."

"Only because you could do so much better."

"We've already covered this territory."

"Then I guess we have nothing left to talk about." Willow consulted the recipe card and set the oven timer.

"Will you go out with me again?"

"No!"

"Why not?"

"We definitely already went over *that* territory."

"So the only reason you won't go out with me is because you can't forgive me for loving you too much?"

"That's an interesting spin on what happened." Oddly enough, the same one Nana used. Had they talked about it? Or had they each come up with that phrase independently? "And it's not the only reason."

"What else is there?" Instantly, he was off his stool and standing before her, gripping her upper arms firmly enough to force her to look into his eyes. "We are incredible together. The evening I spent with you—and not just the sex, but the whole thing—was the most fun I've had in years. It was just like it used to be, only better. And you thought so, too."

She couldn't deny it. They'd always been compatible, at least when it came to their personalities and their interests. But now they had true physical chemistry, as well, which added a whole new dimension to their relationship.

"I don't want to hurt your feelings," she said.

"Darlin', they could not get any more hurt. What's the problem?"

Well, he'd asked for it. "I could not possibly have a relationship with a man who has so much potential and does nothing with it. We wouldn't be compatible in the long run. I once thought you shared my drive and ambition, that you understood me. But apparently you don't."

"My dropping out of vet school bugs you that much, huh?" He let go of her and turned away. "I didn't peg you for a snob."

"I'm not a snob! I would have been happy to date Hank the ranch cowboy."

"Hank?"

"Since I didn't know your name, I made up one for you. I have no problem with jobs that put calluses on a man's hands. What I can't stand is that first you threw my future in a Dumpster. Then you threw yours there, too."

Well, there it was, out in the open. Willow hadn't realized she felt so strongly about Cal's choice of career, or rather his choice not to bother with a career at all. Had she been holding on to her anger over their ill-fated first sexual encounter so that she wouldn't have to face the real problem?

He just stood there for a few moments, his jaw about dragging the floor.

"I guess I've always been slightly jealous of you," she continued, because she really wanted him to understand, and nothing she said now could be worse anyway. "Your natural brilliance, the way everything came so easy for you, the parents who encouraged but never pushed, never punished. Everything just dropped into your lap while I was in an eternal struggle. I managed to contain it for a long time, because I was able to tell myself that you deserved it, you were going to serve humankind with your talents, that sort of thing. But when you turned your back on your brilliant future—"

She stopped when she saw the look in his eye. It was sort of dangerous. He was no longer cajoling.

"I might still have a brilliant future," he said, his voice soft and a little bit scary. She'd never seen him like this before. "Don't count me out yet. Maybe I'm a late bloomer, too." With that he turned and stalked out of the kitchen. Clementine the dog stood and trotted after him.

"Well, that was interesting," Willow murmured. Cal

had sought her out, apparently wanting to mend fences and make a fresh start. Even after the disastrous conclusion to their date the other night, he was still interested in pursuing her.

And what had she done? Jumped all over him for dropping out of vet school, something he'd done three years ago and that really had nothing to do with her. If he hadn't thought she was psycho before, he surely did now.

But she hadn't been able to help herself, because she'd seen something important while he was working with Danny the horse. She'd seen passion. Not sexual passion, but passion for life, passion for animals.

It simply made no sense that Cal had elected not to be a vet, when vet medicine was the tailor-made occupation for him. She knew she'd done the right thing, even if it had hurt him to hear it. She'd *had* to bring it up. And his answer to her question had only confused her further.

CAL WENT HOME that night, unable to get Willow's words out of his head. She thought he was a failure, that he had no ambition, that he had no intention of using his brain to do something worthwhile.

As he lay in bed with one cat wrapped around his head and another curled up on his chest, sleep wouldn't come. Could Willow's indictment be right? Why *hadn't* he done something with his life? When he'd dropped out of vet school, his parents had told him to take his time and think about what he wanted to do. Well, he'd taken his time, all right. More than three years had passed. And he hadn't been in a hurry. He'd thought he had plenty of time to figure things out.

But maybe not as much as he thought. Twenty-six was still young, but as Willow had pointed out, life could change—or end—in the blink of an eye. And so far, he'd accomplished absolutely nothing, and the days and months were ticking by.

He had a pretty good idea what he wanted to do. He wanted to train horses. That was where his strength lay, and the idea of working with horses, or even other animals, every day turned him on like nothing else. But he'd never let himself think too long or too hard about this ambition. To pursue such a career, he would have to give up a steady job for the risky proposition of a solo venture. And after his misstep at vet school, he wasn't eager to risk another failure.

Even if he committed himself to such a future, he had no idea where to start. He knew nothing about starting a business. Should he go back to school and get an MBA? Work as an apprentice to some established trainer? Run an ad in the paper, Trainer for Hire?

He really didn't know. But there was one person who could help him. Willow Marsden was the world's best goal setter. She'd been setting goals, formulating plans, making lists and working around setbacks for as long as he could remember, while he just went with the flow and things came to him.

Maybe that's what he'd been waiting for—some opportunity to fall into his lap—and it hadn't happened…yet.

Well, Willow was just the one to help him devise a plan of action and take the steps to achieve it. It's what she did best.

But would she help him? Cal punched his pillow and thought about it. He suspected she wouldn't be able to resist if he presented it to her as a problem that needed solving. Willow had never in her life turned her back on a problem or a person in need.

"So," ANNE BEGAN as she helped Willow make hamburger patties, another of a camp cook's endless tasks. "What did you and Cal talk about all that time he was in here yesterday?"

Willow had been hoping no one had paid attention to her extended visit with Cal the previous day. But she should have known better. Nothing around here escaped Anne's notice. Besides, Anne had an overdeveloped interest in the love lives of everyone around her. After finding Wade and marrying him despite some pretty tall odds, she'd managed to marry off both of Wade's older brothers and their grandfather the following year. Now that she had immediate family taken care of, no one in Cottonwood was safe from her machinations.

"I don't really remember what we talked about," Willow hedged, though she precisely recalled every word. "You know how bad my memory is." She had confessed her cognitive shortcomings to Wade and Anne before she'd started working here. As her employers, they had a right to know. They'd been sympathetic and supportive, not pitying, as she'd feared.

"You are the biggest liar," Anne said sweetly.

Willow sighed. "If you must know, we rehashed old arguments and started some new ones."

"What could you possibly argue about? Cal seems really easygoing to me. He's gentle with the horses, relates well to kids. And he's soooo cute."

"And he's soooo not right for me. So please stop matchmaking."

Anne held out her greasy hands in a gesture of innocence. "Who, me? I was just pointing out the man's strengths. So what really happened with you two way back when? I've been squeezing every town gossip I can think of, and no one remembers."

"Really?" That surprised Willow. Was it possible she'd exaggerated the events of that summer in her mind? She'd been sure everyone was staring and pointing at her, laughing behind her back about the fool she'd made of herself over Cal and the mess she'd made of her life.

"So give," Anne said. "I'm a firm believer that there is no history, no matter how tragic, that can't be dealt with and overcome. Wade and I have something really sad in our history. We had a miscarriage."

"Oh, Anne, I'm so sorry. I didn't know that. You certainly seem happy now. And you have Olivia."

"We are happy. But it took some effort to get there. Being pregnant the first time really threw my whole life off track. And then I didn't tell Wade, and then he was mad when he found out—it was terrible. But we worked it through."

Now that Anne had confided in her, Willow felt compelled to make a similar confession. So she told the whole, icky story. Only something odd happened. Right in the middle of it, she started laughing. "My father's face…turned so red I thought…he was going to have a stroke," she said between gasps. "And you've never seen two people get dressed so fast."

"And I bet Cal never made faster tracks for the door, either."

"No, actually, he didn't," Willow said, only now recalling this part. "He stayed and took it. He even tried to take all the blame. But, of course, his strategy didn't work."

Anne handed Willow a paper towel to wipe away her tears of laughter, then got one for herself. "Sounds like he was very noble."

"But first he was very horny."

That started the two women into peals of renewed laughter.

"So, that's it?" Anne asked when she could talk. "That's the big, awful secret of your past that's kept you apart all these years?"

"Well, there was a little more to it than that. Cal and I…we conduct our lives differently. There's just no real hope for a future there."

Anne looked at her skeptically. "Having different outlooks doesn't make for a bad relationship. Look at Wade's brother Jon and his wife, Sherry. They're not just two peas from different pods, they're completely different vegetables."

Willow couldn't argue there. Jonathan was quiet, serious, conservative, maybe a little shy. Sherry was outgoing, flamboyant, brash and outspoken. Yet they were both devoted to their kids and each other, and they seemed happy.

"It's not a good time for me to get entangled with someone. I have a lot on my plate."

"A good man can be a help, rather than a hindrance, when life gets tough."

"Anne, please…"

"Okay, okay, 'nuff said. But I do want to warn you. He's going to be here the rest of the week. Things are slow at the ranch, so Jon's lending Cal to us to saddle-break some of our yearlings. He'll be letting some of the campers help him. And he'll be taking his meals here, too."

Oh, great. Just what she needed, a six-foot distraction. Willow struggled to hide her reaction. "What's one more mouth to feed?"

"You don't mind? Really?"

"I imagine he'll stay out of my way."

WILLOW IMAGINED wrong. Cal managed to be underfoot every time she turned around. He showed up before meals to help in the kitchen. He helped her clean up the dishes. He hung out around the campfire at night and told amusing stories to the kids, who seemed fascinated by small-town life.

On the third night, as he helped her pack up the leftovers, she couldn't help commenting. "Aren't there some horses somewhere that need your attention? You spend more time up at the house with me than you do down at the barn."

"I can't work with the horses all the time," he said. "I have to give them some down time, so they won't get sick of me. So they'll look forward to when I return."

She couldn't help smiling as he held the back door open for her. "You have the damnedest ideas about horse training. I always thought breaking horses was about wrestling them into a saddle, then letting them buck you off a few times until they get used to it."

"That's one way to do it. You show 'em who's boss,

make 'em behave 'cause they're afraid of you. You might succeed in riding the horse, but you'll never be able to trust him."

Willow took out the plastic wrap for the leftover lettuce, tomato and onion. "So that's not how you do it."

"No. I make friends with them, so they trust me and want to please me. It takes a few days, but the first time I get on their backs, they don't buck. They just look surprised."

Willow laughed, picturing the scene. "Here, make yourself useful. Seal up those chip bags and put them in the pantry."

"It's good to hear you laugh."

She used to laugh a lot, when she and Cal were dating. When had she become so serious?

"Come out for a ride with me," he said impulsively. "The moon's almost full."

"I have work to do here."

"I'll help you." He put away the hamburger and hot dog buns while she wiped off the counters.

"Waffles and fresh fruit are on tomorrow's menu. I have a lot of prep work to do."

"I'll help you," he repeated.

"Cal, if I go for a moonlight ride with you, I will do things I regret."

"Really?" he asked hopefully.

She shook her head. How had the man gotten past her defenses? She'd put up brick walls against Cal Chandler years ago, periodically fortifying them by stockpiling evidence against him, keeping her memories of his transgressions alive. But somehow he'd wriggled through a chink in that wall.

Maybe it hadn't even happened tonight. Maybe it had happened three days ago when she'd finally been able to laugh about her unpleasant deflowering. Or earlier, when she'd watched Cal with Danny.

"Okay, okay," Cal tried again. "I'll make a deal with you. You come riding with me and I promise not to touch you or even talk about us dating."

Then what's your point? She almost asked the question out loud. But that would have revealed more about her intentions than his.

He answered almost as if she'd gone ahead and asked. "I have an ulterior motive. I need your mind."

Now it was getting thick! "*My* mind? You're the one who made straight *A*s and had perfect SAT scores."

"Yeah, but you're the one who sets goals and solves strategic problems. And that's the sort of critical thinking I require."

Willow was intrigued despite herself. What sort of critical thinking did Cal need? If he had some problem at the ranch or with the horses, there were many more knowledgeable people he could ask than her. Besides, since the accident her brain wasn't exactly at its best and brightest.

But she couldn't resist the challenge.

"All right. You help me by cutting up the fruit for tomorrow, and I'll lend you my brain, such as it is. But let's forget the horseback riding. Critical thinking requires brainstorming, and that requires paper and pen. We can go back to Nana's and spread out in the den."

"Deal."

Then she just realized what she'd done. She'd invited him over. Late at night. It was almost like…a date.

Chapter Seven

Nana was still up watching a movie when Willow arrived home, slightly breathless. She was grateful Nana wasn't like most grandmothers. She didn't go to bed early. She was a night owl who especially liked staying up to watch Letterman—which made her a darn good chaperone.

And that was what Willow needed right now. What had she been thinking, inviting Cal to come over this late at night? She'd taken pains to indicate it wasn't a date, but she knew it would feel like one if she didn't work at it.

He had promised not to touch her. But she had made no such promise. He probably had more to worry about than she did.

"I've lost my mind and invited Cal to come over," she announced as soon as she came in the door. "I told him I'd help him with a project."

Nana shot out of her recliner, simultaneously switching off the TV right in the middle of the weather update. "This is wonderful. I'll get out the cookies, and—"

"No, no. Don't do anything special. This isn't a date.

You don't have to disappear—in fact, I don't want you to disappear. We won't be waiting for you to go to bed so we can make out. I'm just helping him with something."

"I'm pleased to see you're talking with him again. Does this mean—"

"It doesn't mean anything," Willow said coolly, "except that I realized it's stupid to hold a grudge for all these years, and I've made myself get over it."

"Good for you."

"We're not dating. I don't have time to date. I'm leaving for med school in three weeks and I have enough complications in my life without developing some adolescent crush on a guy."

"Methinks the lady doth protest too—"

"Don't start with me." Willow folded her arms and glared.

Nana started to protest further, but the front doorbell rang. She flashed what could only be described as a triumphant smile. "I'll get that. You fix your hair," she admonished. "Put on some lipstick."

Willow sighed. Her grandmother hadn't heard a word past *I've invited Cal to come over.* Nonetheless, Willow peeked at herself in a hall mirror and realized she did look something of a mess. Caving in to a bit of feminine vanity, she ducked into the bathroom, took her hair down from its coiled braid and ran a brush through it, and put some clear gloss on her lips.

They were dry from the hot weather, she reasoned. And she wasn't primping. She was simply maintaining reasonable hygienic standards.

By the time she emerged, Cal was already in the kitchen—eating from the always-ready supply of cookies in the cookie jar. He knew where to find them. Nana was pouring him a glass of milk.

"Willow, Cal is here," Nana said superfluously. "Do you want some milk, too?"

"No, thanks, I'm still full from dinner. Hi, Cal. We can work in here at the table, since Nana's watching TV in the den."

Nana yawned elaborately. "Oh, no, dear, I'm going right to bed. Just can't stay up late like I used to. You two have fun." She pulled a disappearing act worthy of a magician's rabbit.

Willow shrugged. "She can't help herself. She wants us to be like we were in the old days. Maybe because she's feeling her age."

Cal grinned. "I don't think that's it. I could say something, but I promised I wouldn't."

"Oh, you're just hoping I'll beg you to say it anyway. No, no, we're not playing that game." She found a legal pad and pen in the cabinet under the kitchen wall phone. "We might as well work in the kitchen, anyway, since we're already here." She sat down at the table across from him, pen in hand, poised. "So, shoot. What are you working on?"

Cal seemed resigned to actually getting down to business. "I started thinking about what you said. About how I'm throwing away my future and not living up to my potential and all that."

She cringed, hearing her harsh words thrown back at her. Still, she wouldn't retract them. They'd needed to be said.

"I've decided you're right," he continued. "The last three years, I've just been treading water, waiting for an opportunity to present itself, the way it always did for me in the past. But this time, it didn't."

She waited, sensing he was on to something important. Whatever it was he wanted to talk about, it mattered a great deal to him. He seemed uncharacteristically hesitant about revealing whatever it was.

"So," he continued, "I started asking myself some questions. About what I really wanted. And the answer was pretty easy. I want to be a horse trainer. Full-time. Helping out occasionally with Wade's horses just makes me hungry to do more."

Willow was honestly delighted. She wasn't imagining things. She *had* seen something in Cal's face that afternoon, some hint that he'd been engaged in the work he was meant to do. "I think that's wonderful," she said without reservation.

"So how do I do it? I thought of trying to get on with someone established. But—"

"No *but*s right now." Willow could feel Cal's excitement and anticipation, and it was contagious. "I know nothing about horse training, but I know brainstorming. We'll write down as many ideas about becoming a horse trainer as we can. Then we'll evaluate them later."

She was in her element now. She loved this kind of thing. For half an hour, she and Cal threw out ideas, everything from running ads in the paper to joining the circus to getting a government grant to tame wild mustangs. She scribbled furiously in the legal pad, elated to discover that this part of her brain worked just fine. Occasionally she threw out an idea that had already been discussed only minutes earlier, proving her memory was still short-circuiting. But instead of panicking when it happened, she just tossed aside her lapses with an "Oh, sorry," and they went on.

They worked in perfect harmony, two minds with one purpose. They drew charts, made lists, asked questions, moving from brainstorming to generating a workable plan as they determined which areas of the concept required further research and which could be acted upon right away.

At last, Willow happened to glance at the clock and she gasped. "Cal, it's two o'clock in the morning!"

He grinned. "Don't worry, I won't get in trouble for missing my curfew."

"I have to get up in four hours." She couldn't believe she'd gotten so carried away. But she'd had fun, she realized. Helping someone else figure out his dream and how to live it was almost as good as living her own dream. Especially when that person was Cal.

How could she have believed he was without ambition? He had real passion. All he'd needed was a goal tailor-made for the passion, and he was off like a rocket. With her help—

Whoa. This was a one-time deal, she reminded herself. As interesting as she found the prospect of starting a horse-training venture, it was Cal's deal, not hers. She had other priorities.

"I guess I better get going." His reluctance was obvious. "I've got to squeeze in a trip to the library tomorrow, so I need to get an early start."

"And I'll call the Pattersons for you." Her mother had mentioned that their neighbor's Shetland pony had gone berserk during the recent tornado and now couldn't be touched. That sounded like a job custom-made for Cal.

She wondered if other horses in the area had been traumatized by the storm.

"And the Internet search?" he asked hopefully.

"Oh, right." She wrote that down on her follow-up list, then also added it to the notebook around her neck. She'd promised to do a search of other horse trainers in the area to see what sorts of Web sites they had, if any, and how they marketed themselves to the public. "I can use Wade's computer after breakfast. I'm sure he won't mind."

Cal stood and gathered up the stack of papers they generated, as well as a couple of motivational books Willow was lending him. "I really don't know how to thank you for this, Willow. I was hoping maybe I'd get a ten-minute pep talk, some reassurance that I wasn't crazy for wanting to do this. I never expected you to put in all this work."

"It'll be thanks enough if you make this thing work. Besides, I had fun."

"I'll make it work. I'll talk to both Jon and Wade tomorrow about referrals. I just hope Jon doesn't decide to fire me when he finds out I want to do something else besides herd Hardison cattle."

"He won't. He'll want to help. Everyone wants to be part of a dream, especially a big, exciting dream like this one." She stood, too, intending to walk him to the door.

"Do you really think it's exciting? Or is it just a pipe dream?"

She could hear the emotion in his voice. This was so important to him that he was afraid to commit to it totally just in case it didn't come true. If he let fear block him, he would never take those first, crucial steps toward achieving his dream. "Exciting and very doable," she told him. "You have a unique approach to horse training. You've built a better mousetrap. The world is going to beat a path to your door. You have to believe in yourself for this to work."

"I'll believe in me if you will."

That was when Willow realized she was in trouble. She hadn't just signed on for a few hours of brainstorming. She was in on the ground floor of an immense undertaking. She'd become part and parcel to Cal's dream.

Oh, hell.

HE WAS GOING to kiss her. No, he wasn't, damn it. Like a fool, he'd promised he wouldn't lay a hand on her this evening if she helped him. And he did not break promises. Ever.

Then he realized it was a moot point, because Willow was kissing him. Yeah, that's what really happened, he thought dazedly. She threw her arms around his neck and planted one right on his mouth, surprising the bejabers out of him.

The pile of papers he'd held in one hand fluttered to the floor like autumn leaves. Kissing Willow was like a long-forgotten dream. He thought he remembered what it felt like when he wasn't with her. Then when she was in his arms, he realized his memory didn't do her justice at all.

The kiss was short for all its intensity. Willow pulled away first, out of breath, her face slightly flushed. "Oh, my God, what am I doing?"

"Don't panic on me, Willow. It was just a kiss."

She pulled away even farther, sliding her arms down his shoulders, taking a step back. "I didn't mean for that to happen. I just got caught up in all the excitement."

"I'm not complaining."

"But I'm sending you mixed signals. I...I don't know what I want. I know what I *should* want, but..."

"This doesn't have to mean anything." It was a blatant lie. It meant a lot to him, having her kiss him, especially since this time she knew exactly whom she was kissing. He would be up the other half of the night, pondering what was going on with her. But she didn't have to know that. "A kiss between friends, okay?"

"It's just that—"

"Willow, listen to me. Tonight, you showed me how to do what you do best—planning, preparing, being logical. Now let me give you a little advice about what I do best—living in the moment. Stop obsessing about the past and worrying about the future. Enjoy the here and now."

He touched her chin, gently turning her head until she had to look at him again.

"That was a very nice kiss. Thank you again." He kissed her on the cheek, then her forehead. "Now go get some sleep. I'll let myself out."

It almost killed him to pick up his papers, then turn and walk away when he knew she was receptive to him, knew her hormones were racing through her veins right now, confusing the heck out of her. He could take advantage of that confusion, but he had made that mistake once and was still paying for it. Instead, he hoped he was leaving her wanting more.

WILLOW WOKE early the next morning after a poor couple of hours of sleep. She showered and dressed quickly, braided her hair, then quietly slipped out of the bathroom, hoping she could get out of the house before her grandmother woke. She wasn't feeling up to Nana's questions this morning. Her grandmother would want to know all about her visit with Cal and the project they'd worked on until two in the morning. And Nana *would* know exactly what time Cal left last night. She was a light sleeper.

But Nana was already up. The coffee was brewing, and she was assembling the ingredients for some baked treat.

"You're up awfully early," Willow commented as she snitched half a cup of half-brewed coffee. A few swallows were all she needed to wake herself up enough to drive to the camp.

"I went to bed so early last night that my eyes popped open at the crack of dawn."

"I can't believe you bailed out on me after I asked you to stick around," Willow scolded, though there was no real bite to the remark. "Mmm, blueberry muffins?"

"No. The blueberries at Grubbs' were too pricey. I'm thinking of banana bread."

"Even better. I'll have some later. I've got to run. I'm making waffles this morning for the kiddos."

"You're going to race out the door without telling me what happened with Cal?" Nana asked, sounding distressed.

"Have to. Don't worry, you can interrogate me tonight when I get home."

"Just tell me one thing. Did he kiss you?"

"Nana!"

"He did, he did!" she crowed.

Willow sighed. "The truth? He was a perfect gentleman. I'm the bad one. I kissed him. I went completely out of my mind."

"Nothing wrong with that. If you can't go crazy over a man, what *can* you go crazy over?"

Willow smiled despite herself. "I have to scoot. See you tonight."

AFTER THE WAFFLE and fruit salad breakfast extravaganza and cleanup, Willow had all of thirty minutes free before she had to start lunch preparations. She consulted her notebook, which had become her lifeline, and recalled the tasks she'd promised to perform for Cal.

Instead of the surge of excitement she felt last night, she felt a stab of apprehension. What if she was encouraging Cal to pursue the wrong dream? What if, like vet school, he spent a lot of time and money on this venture and then realized that it was wrong, too? What did she know about horse training, after all? Maybe she should have tried to talk him into returning to vet school.

Her doubts whirled around her head as she used Wade's computer to search the Internet for other horse trainers in the area. She found very few, and the ones who did have an Internet presence seemed to be traditional workhorse and rodeo trainers. She didn't find any nearby who dealt with animal behavior problems, which was where she and Cal had determined his focus should be. That, at least, was encouraging.

Next, she called the Pattersons about their traumatized pony.

"I don't think I know Cal Chandler," Mrs. Patterson

said in her deep, smoker's voice. "Is he someone your parents know?"

Oh, Lord, Willow didn't want Mrs. Patterson going to *them* for a recommendation. Cal wasn't exactly high on their list.

"He's Old Doc Chandler's grandson and Winn Chandler's son," Willow said, figuring everyone knew one or the other of the best-known vets working in the tri-county area. "He works for the Hardison Ranch."

"I appreciate your trying to help," Mrs. Patterson said, "and I'm sure this young man is wonderful, but Pepper won't let anyone near him, not even my daughter. And they're deeply bonded."

"Please, Mrs. Patterson, just let him try." Willow didn't want to sound desperate, but she knew that if anyone could help, Cal could.

"Well, if you'll come out with him. My husband doesn't like letting strangers near our animals."

"I, um, okay," Willow agreed without much enthusiasm. She'd been planning to perform the tasks she'd promised Cal she would do, then extricate herself from his plans. Much as she wanted to see Cal succeed, she had her own future to think about. She'd been putting off her own trip to the library to do some research on cognitive impairments. Though her neurologist had assured Willow she was doing everything that could be done, she wasn't so sure. Maybe there was some type of therapy, an exercise or a drug, that could speed things up.

Less than three weeks until she was supposed to show up at med school, and there was no way she would be able to handle the demands given her current abilities. Or rather, lack of abilities.

CAL DIDN'T WANT to admit it, but he was nervous as he drove Highway 17 toward Mooresville. Doing a favor for Wade Hardison was one thing. Saddle-breaking young quarter horses was something he could do in his sleep.

But approaching a strange, dysfunctional pony owned by people he'd never met and who might be expecting miracles— Well, it was just scary.

He was glad Willow had come with him, though she was strangely quiet in the passenger seat of his truck. She'd brought some books with her, which she intended to study while he worked. One book, a fat medical text, was called *An Introduction to Cognitive Dysfunction.* Another was some type of workbook for children.

"So you didn't discuss my fee with the Pattersons?" Wade asked.

"No."

"I'm still not sure what to charge. But maybe the initial assessment should be free. I won't know anything until I see the horse."

"You could do it that way," Willow agreed. "Then give an estimate based on how long you think it will take to solve the problem."

"My estimate might be really high or really low."

"You're going to make some mistakes at first. It'll take some practice before you figure out the best way to charge for your services."

There was something in Willow's voice that bothered Cal. She seemed a lot more distant than she had the other night during their planning session. A lot less enthusiastic.

"Have you decided this whole thing is a bad idea after all?" he asked.

"What? No, of course not. The Pattersons are very influential in Mooresville. Do a good job for them and they'll recommend you around town."

"I mean, the whole horse trainer thing. Now that you've had a chance to think about it."

"No, I still think it's a great idea."

"You just seem kind of...withdrawn."

She was silent for a few moments, and he could tell she was weighing her words.

"Come on, Willow, spit it out."

"Okay, here's the deal. I'm so excited about your venture that I actually get giddy. I keep thinking about it, jotting down ideas. And mostly I'm excited because you're excited."

"You don't act excited."

"That's because I'm trying not to get too involved. It's so tempting to throw myself into this with both feet, devote all my spare time and brain power to helping you make it work. But I have other commitments."

"You mean the camp? You cleared it with Anne, didn't you?"

"Not the camp. I should be studying right now. I should be reviewing class notes. I should be researching prosopagnosia at the library instead of checking out horse trainer's Web sites. I should be doing everything possible to prepare myself for med school."

"Proso—what?"

"Prosopagnosia. It's the medical term for face-blindness."

"I thought you were getting better."

"I'm learning to disguise the problem, that's all. But you didn't see me this morning. I got so many names wrong at breakfast, one of the counselors thought I was on drugs."

"But you know me."

"You just think I do. When you walked up to me at the pavilion earlier, I thought you were Wade again. But I've learned to keep my mouth shut until I get some cue that clues me in. In your case, it's your voice."

Cal was stunned. "Wade and I don't look anything alike."

She shrugged. "Cowboy hats, cowboy boots, blue jeans, six feet with broad shoulders. That's what I have to work with."

It was like a kick in the gut, acknowledging the fact that Willow still couldn't tell him apart from her employer. "I don't mean to monopolize your time," he finally said. "But I don't see how studying about the face-blindness is going to solve it. It's not like studying for a test."

"I figure the more I exercise my memory, the better it'll get. When you learn stuff, you create connections between brain neurons. Maybe it's just a matter of re-establishing those neural synapses."

"I don't think it works like that."

"Well, I can't just sit around and do nothing!"

"You aren't. You're helping me." But he could see that wasn't the answer she wanted.

"Maybe your brain needs to rest rather than work. Sometimes healing requires inactivity."

Willow shook her head. "It's hard to explain, but it almost feels like all the memories are there, all the working parts are there, and that it just needs to be shaken up or worked loose in order to work perfectly again."

His heart dropped. Only last night, Willow had tried to explain her problem to him, using almost those exact words. She'd repeated herself at other times, too, but he'd tried to tell himself everybody did that.

Deep down, though, he knew that wasn't the case. Willow's short-term memory lapses were pretty serious, and probably more of a threat to her aspirations than even the face-blind thing.

No wonder she didn't seem overwhelmed with joy.

He turned onto the street where Willow had grown up, in a bucolic neighborhood where the houses sat on a couple of acres each and everybody owned horses. The street had a country feel to it, though it was less than two miles from the center of town.

He felt a little odd, returning here to the scene of the crime, so to speak. He'd hardly seen or spoken to Willow's parents since the embarrassing incident. He'd seen them at the store once, and they'd spoken to him civilly, if a little stiffly. But then, Willow's parents had never been the warm, fuzzy types, so he didn't know if they still held a grudge against him for deflowering their daughter.

At any rate, they were probably safely at work at the bank this afternoon, so he didn't have to worry about running into them.

Willow directed him to the house on the far side of hers.

"I haven't seen the Pattersons in a long time," she said, sounding a bit nervous.

She was probably worried she wouldn't recognize them.

Before they could even get out of the truck, a large, square-shouldered woman in baggy jeans and a work shirt bustled out the front door and straight up to Willow. Cal had intended to introduce himself quickly so Willow wouldn't have to—on the off chance that this was not Mrs. Patterson. But he didn't get the chance.

"Willow, it's so good to see you," the woman said in a deep, gravelly voice. "Your mother told me all about your accident. You're looking wonderful."

"Thanks, Mr. Patterson. You look good, too."

The woman's face froze. "I'm Mrs. Patterson," she said flatly.

"What? Well, of course you are. What did I say?" Willow did a good job of acting bewildered, as if she hadn't just mistaken the missus for the mister. Granted, the woman's appearance was slightly androgynous and her voice deep for a woman, but…oh, poor Willow. Here he was, all excited about his dreams, and Willow was facing the fact that the dreams she'd held forever were coming unraveled.

Chapter Eight

Mrs. Patterson recovered. "You just misspoke, Willow, that's all," she said, glossing over the awkward moment. But Willow's face was as red as her shirt. She knew what she'd done.

"And this must be Cal," Mrs. Patterson said.

Cal shook the woman's hand. Then she wasted no time showing them to a small corral in back, where a black-and-white Shetland pony stood on the far side next to the fence. Small even for a pony, it looked skinny and unkempt, with mud on its shaggy coat and knots in its long tail.

"I know he looks awful," Mrs. Patterson said, sounding embarrassed. "But we haven't been able to get near him even to groom him. He's always been such a dear little thing. All my children have outgrown him, but we can't bear the thought of selling him."

The "dear little thing" peered at them with malevolent eyes. It shook its head, as if warning Cal off.

"During the storm, the roof blew off Pepper's stall and landed inside," Mrs. Patterson went on to explain. "He was pinned inside against a wall. When my husband got him free, he went crazy, absolutely crazy. Now if anyone tries to approach him, he runs and kicks. And he puts down his head and shakes it like a bull ready to charge."

Cal didn't have much experience with Shetlands. He'd known one when he was a kid, a cream-colored mare with the inappropriate name of Buttercup, who was notorious for kicking and biting. But horses were horses, right? He climbed over the fence and entered Pepper's domain.

"Be careful, Cal," Mrs. Patterson said. "He's little, but he kicks like the devil."

Cal didn't doubt it. Even as small as he was, Pepper easily outweighed Cal. Cal made no immediate attempts to approach the pony, but instead walked along the fence, as if he had his own agenda. The pony watched, tense, ears forward, listening.

Eventually Cal's path led him closer to the pony. When he saw its muscles bunch, as if it was ready to flee, he changed direction.

Sensing no threat, the pony grew more interested in Cal's seemingly odd behavior.

After about fifteen minutes of this, the pony decided to approach Cal. But when he got close, Cal waved him away. *I don't want to play with you.*

To a horse, this was the worst possible insult. An animal with a herding instinct, no horse wanted to be told he can't join the herd, even if it's a herd of one human.

Cal soon had Pepper trotting around the corral in a circle. He watched for some signs that the horse was willing to acquiesce to Cal's dominance. They came pretty quickly. Head down. Licking and chewing its lips. One ear cocked, listening.

Cal then turned his body slightly, indicating in horse

language he was now open to being approached. And
sure enough, Pepper walked up to him, completely trust-
ing, wanting to make friends.

Cal pulled a carrot stick from his jeans pocket and
offered it to Pepper. The pony took it eagerly, but just
as quickly spit it out on the ground. Cal could see frustration in the pony's eyes.

And something else: pain. It was hard to describe exactly what that expression was, but it had something to
do with tension around the eyes and lips. He scratched
Pepper's forelock, then walked over to where Mrs. Patterson stood on the fence, watching.

"That is amazing," she said. "Look at him. Docile as
a lamb."

Pepper followed behind Cal, heeling like a dog, eager
for more attention.

"I can't thank you enough—" Mrs. Patterson started
to say, as if his job was over.

"Wait, I'm not done. Has Pepper been eating well?"

"Oh, no, that's the other thing. He hardly touches
his oats."

Cal was pretty sure Pepper's problem was organic, and
not psychological trauma. He started with the most obvious theory, that Pepper had suffered a head injury when
the stall roof fell on him. Thinking of head injuries made
him think of Willow. Maybe Pepper didn't recognize his
family anymore, and that's why he was so freaked out!

But once Pepper let Cal get a look inside his mouth,
he immediately saw the problem. He gave the horse a
parting pat and returned to Mrs. Patterson and Willow.
"One of his teeth is broken off at the root, and now it's
abscessed. It probably hurts like hell."

"But his behavior started so abruptly after the storm," Mrs. Patterson argued.

"He might have gotten hit in the jaw when the stall roof fell in. It could have made a slight problem worse. A vet will have to sedate him and pull the tooth. But that should solve the problem."

Cal opened the corral gate and allowed Mrs. Patterson inside. Pepper flicked his ears, but showed no other sign of distress as Mrs. Patterson petted his neck. "It's okay, Pepper," she crooned. "I'll get Doc Chandler over here and get you fixed up." She was almost in tears at the thought of her beloved pony in pain.

Cal smiled, glad he was able to help. He didn't know for sure that the pony would remain calm until the dental problem was solved, but for now Pepper seemed confident that no one was going to hurt him further.

"I'll go inside and get my checkbook," Mrs. Patterson said, giving the pony a final pat. "How much do I owe you?"

Cal had been dreading this question. Before he could formulate an answer, Willow piped up.

"Cal normally charges a hundred dollars for a house call, plus a hundred an hour. But since you're a good friend of my parents—"

"I'll be right back."

As soon as Mrs. Patterson was out of earshot, Cal exploded. "That's too much money!"

"I was going to give her a discount. But she cut me off."

"A hundred dollars an hour?"

"That's what any professional charges. Lawyers, doctors—"

"I'm not a lawyer or a doctor. Or a vet."

"Don't undervalue yourself. It was a long drive over here."

Mrs. Patterson soon reappeared and handed Cal a folded check. "Worth every penny. I'm going to call your grandfather right now."

Cal didn't look at the check until he and Willow were in the truck. It wasn't for two hundred dollars. It was three hundred.

He grinned. His first professional consulting fee. The grin grew into a triumphant hoot. "I'm taking you out to dinner at Bremond's." Bremond's was a premiere steakhouse in nearby Tyler and the most expensive restaurant in three counties.

"No, you're not," Willow said sensibly. "You're going straight to the bank to open a special business account, and you're going to set aside twenty-five percent for taxes."

"Aw, you take all the fun out of it. How about a pulled-pig sandwich at Triple G Barbecue?"

"I have to get back to work."

"You're serious about this," he said, sobering. "You're going to shut me out."

"I have challenges ahead of me. You just saw exactly how far I have to go. I thought Mrs. Patterson was her husband."

"I still say studying and obsessing over the problem won't make it go away."

"I'm not obsessing. I'm focusing. There's a difference."

WILLOW WAS determined to stay away from Cal during the few days that remained of this session of the rodeo camp. She threw herself into her work, hanging out with the kids whenever she got a break from cooking.

She practiced figuring out the kids' identities from a distance and memorizing visual cues besides clothes, which could change at any time. She realized people's ears could be distinctive. Jan, one of the counselors, had five piercings in one ear. Willow got to where she could identify her instantly. And while Wade and Cal were particularly difficult for her to tell apart, she finally realized their walks were very different. Wade had a longer stride, and he swung his arms. Cal's walk was smoother, with less twisting of the shoulders.

Whenever she spotted a cowboy with that gliding, graceful walk, she walked the other way.

Anne mentioned that she'd heard of the miracle Cal had pulled with Pepper the pony, and that two of the Pattersons' friends had called Cal the very next day. One had a horse he'd bought at an auction that had a kicking problem. Another had a dog that wouldn't come out from under the house.

"And did Cal help?" Willow asked, trying to sound casual, though she was dying to know how Cal was coming with his change of career.

"The kicking horse will require several sessions, but I'm sure he can cure the problem. He's dealt successfully with kicking before."

"What about the dog?"

Anne laughed. "She was having puppies. Cal managed to wiggle part way under the house, snag one of the pups with a loop of rope, and pull it out. The mother dog grabbed a second puppy and followed. Then she moved the whole brood to the back porch. Problem solved."

"He should have gotten combat pay for that one.

He's lucky mama dog didn't take his arm off at the shoulder."

"I know. Can you imagine, grubbing around under someone's dirty house? There were probably mice and stuff." Anne gave a delicate shiver.

"I can imagine Cal doing it," Willow said, "if there was an animal involved. Do you know that he accidentally ran over a snake in his driveway and then he rescued it? Took it inside, put it in the bathtub, nursed it back to health."

Anne laughed again. "A man with a soft heart. Oh, Willow, he is something special. You're not going to let him get away, are you?"

"I don't need a boyfriend."

"If you say you're too busy, I'm going to scream. *No one* is too busy for love. Don't put it off like I did. I was so focused on being a high-powered attorney that I almost let the best man in the world slip past me. What if you delay until it's too late? What if Cal is your one-in-a-million, and by the time you're ready for a boyfriend it's too late and he's found someone else?"

Willow waved away Anne's concerns. "I don't believe there's only one perfect partner for each person." But she couldn't deny that the thought of Cal married to some other woman, raising that woman's children, teaching them to ride and train horses, was a little disconcerting.

The fact was, in all the years they'd been apart, she'd never heard that Cal dated anyone else. She assumed he did while he was at school in another city. But she was glad she'd never had to witness it firsthand—Cal in line at the movies, his arm around the waist of some pretty thing, someone more easygoing, someone who didn't always have her nose to the grindstone.

"You know what?" Willow said suddenly, slapping her book closed. "I'm a drudge."

"Oh, now, I wouldn't go that far."

"It's true. I don't know how to have fun. I can't remember the last time I went to a movie." Of course, she couldn't enjoy a movie in her current state. She wasn't able to keep the characters straight, and by the time she got to the end she would have forgotten what went on at the beginning.

"Does this sudden self-discovery have anything to do with Cal?"

"Maybe." She looked at Anne, a wild idea taking hold of her psyche. "What if I let down my guard and spent some time with Cal, got to know him again, put the past behind me?"

"I think it would be the smartest thing you could do," Anne said point-blank.

"You, Nana, Cal—you've all been telling me the same thing. And I thought you were all wrong. But maybe I'm the one who sees everything cockeyed. I am the one with scrambled brains, after all."

"Sometimes other people can see our situations more clearly than we can ourselves," Anne said diplomatically. But her green eyes sparkled with mischief. "Cal is working with the yearlings this morning. Do it now, before you change your mind."

Willow stood. "Okay. Okay, I will."

WILLOW REFUSED to let herself think too hard as she marched out of the house and down to the corrals. The kids were using the large practice ring, preparing for the rodeo finale tomorrow. Parents, teachers, counselors and social workers would be on hand to watch the children demonstrate their newly acquired horsemanship skills. Wade would pass out ribbons and trophies like candy.

"Is Cal around?" Willow asked Jan, who was adjusting a saddle for a ten-year-old girl named Freddi.

"In the barn, I think. The babies are getting shoes today."

"The babies" were what everyone called the yearlings, though they were full-grown horses.

Willow wandered into the cavernous barn. Gary Aimes, the blacksmith, was indeed there. A pretty bay horse named Latte stood in the wide passageway having the equine equivalent of a pedicure. Cal stood next to the mare, scratching her under her chin and apparently deep in conversation with her. The muscle-bound blacksmith had Latte's foreleg between his knees, tapping the nails into a shiny new shoe.

Willow stood back, waiting until Gary finished before approaching. Latte was a bit skittish, from what Willow had seen, and she didn't want to cause problems.

Once the last nail was in, Gary released the horse's leg. "I don't know what you did to calm her down," Gary said with a laugh, "but it sure worked."

"He speaks horse," Willow said as she walked up slowly, still cautious about startling the horse. But Latte did seem unusually calm. She didn't mind when Willow stroked her neck.

"It's just a matter of trust," Cal said. "Hi, Willow. Do you know Gary?"

"By reputation."

They made a bit of small talk as Gary packed up the tools of his trade. Latte was apparently the last horse that needed shoes. He soon departed, leaving Cal and Willow alone.

"I have to take Latte out to the pasture. Did you need something? I'm not staying for dinner, if you're trying to get a head count."

Willow was a bit disappointed to hear that. "It's our last campfire cookout. The kids'll be going home tomorrow after the rodeo."

"I know. But I have to drive into Tyler. I'm buying a computer."

"Really?" She walked alongside him as he led Latte out the barn door.

"If I'm going to make this business thing work, I'll need business cards, invoices, flyers. In the long run, it'll be a lot cheaper and more efficient if I can print those things myself. And I need a Web site. I'm gonna hire a college kid to design one for me and teach me how to update it."

"Oh, I know someone who would be perfect. My old roommate's brother—"

"Willow. Stop." He opened a gate leading to a grassy pasture where several other horses were grazing. After unclipping the lead from Latte's halter, he sent the horse into the pasture with an affectionate slap on the rump.

"You already have someone in mind?"

"No. I mean, you said you were done with me. You said you needed to pull back. You have your own agenda, your own goals, and I understand if you don't want to get all involved helping with mine. But I was just getting used to the idea that I could do this alone. So don't start throwing me names and offering advice if you're going to turn around and snub me again."

"Snub you? Is that what you think I did?"

He pushed his hair off his forehead in an impatient gesture. "No. I think you thought it through and made a decision based on your needs, which is a perfectly sensible and logical thing to do. I don't think you did it to hurt me or make me mad. In fact, I don't think you thought much about me at all. Because it's always about you, isn't it?"

Willow took a step back. This was a side of Cal she'd rarely seen. He hardly ever spoke to her with irritation, much less anger in his voice. Even the other day, when they'd argued about his lack of ambition, his tone had been more…challenging.

"You look at every situation from every angle," he continued, "weigh your decision based on how it will affect you. And when something doesn't go your way, you agonize over how your plan went wrong and then you scramble to alter your strategy and minimize the damage.

"But do you ever stop to think about the fallout to everybody around you?"

Willow was so shocked by this unwarranted attack, she couldn't even find words to defend herself. She just stood there staring, her throat tightening, her eyes burning. What had happened to her Cal, her sweet, kind Cal?

"You say that what happened five years ago totally messed up your life. But did you ever once think about how it messed up mine?"

"It didn't mess up yours. You went on to finish school and attend vet school, just like you'd planned."

"Yeah, but that was after I had to go home and tell my parents what I'd done. I couldn't look my mother in the eye for a year. I still don't think she's forgiven me for losing you. You were as much a daughter to her as my own sister."

Cal was right, Willow thought, feeling about six inches tall. She had shared a wonderful relationship with Marilyn Chandler. But after the breakup, she'd cut herself off from Cal's family, too.

"I didn't know your parents were upset with you. I always figured you could do no wrong in their eyes."

"They didn't cut me off at the knees like your parents did to you. They tried to understand, and I think they did. But it was rough going for a while. And then—" He stopped himself.

"What?"

"Never mind."

"No, tell me. I guess I need to know."

"It's just that, well, maybe the reason I dropped out of vet school had something to do with you, too."

Willow was stunned. "Me? But I was nowhere near you."

"Exactly. It wasn't the same," he said. "Nothing was the same after we broke up. Without you cheering me on, without you to share my successes with, vet school just didn't matter anymore. And I had other plans, too, that I had to toss out the window."

"What plans?"

"The house in the suburbs, the picket fence, two-point-two kids. I planned to marry you. I'd have married you then, if I thought it would fix things."

All the breath whooshed out of Willow. She'd had no idea. Yes, they'd been in love, the passionate, teenage version of it. But they'd never talked about *marriage*.

And if Cal had brought it up, it probably would have scared her to pieces.

A lot of things scared her back then.

One thing scared her now. She'd blown it with Cal. He was right; he was so totally right. She was completely self-involved. She *did* always look at everything in terms of how it affected her. She'd been fighting for herself for so long now, it had become a habit, and not always a very good one.

Her father had said something to that effect at lunch a couple of weeks ago—something about how she enjoyed all the focus being on her—but she'd dismissed it as nonsense.

Maybe her father had had a point.

"I'm sorry, Cal." She was appalled to realize she'd never said that to him. "I'm sorry I hurt you. You're right. I'm a selfish twit. And I haven't changed or grown up at all. Thirty minutes ago, when I made the decision to come talk to you, all I considered was what would be right for *me,* what would work out best for *my* plans. I didn't even stop to consider whether it would be fair to you."

"Whether what would be fair? What are you talking about?"

Willow's face burned. She couldn't tell him now. What she'd been about to propose to him was horrendous. "No, never mind. It was a bad idea."

She turned and fled as if she were being chased by killer bees.

Chapter Nine

Cal watched Willow go and he felt like sticking his head in the watering trough. What had he been thinking? He never lost his temper, never went off on tirades. And to aim his frustrations at Willow, when all she'd done was make a friendly suggestion, was really out of character for him.

But she'd really hit a nerve. First, she'd thrown herself into his project with all the enthusiasm and passion he knew was in her. Then, she abruptly pulled back, completely oblivious to the fact that she'd stomped all over his heart yet again.

Then, just as blithely she'd come back, like a yo-yo with a mind of its own, all friendly and smiling. She really had no idea what she did to him. She had no clue how much it hurt to even look at her and know he couldn't touch her, and how the soft sound of her voice tickled every nerve ending in his body.

Suddenly, it had just gotten to him. And before he knew what was happening, he was spewing all the anger and frustration and bitterness he'd never expressed before.

Hell, maybe he hadn't even known it was there. He'd told himself he quit vet school because he'd realized it wasn't the right fit for him, and that's what he'd always believed. He'd explained to his family that he'd realized he didn't want to deal with sick and injured animals all of the time. It was too painful.

His dropping out had nothing to do with Willow. Except maybe it did. With Willow there to encourage him, he might have worked through his doubts and stuck with it. But without her, everything had seemed so lackluster, even the career he'd been groomed for his whole life.

Still, it had been his decision to quit. Blaming Willow was just plain not right. He'd been lashing out and had said the one thing he knew would hurt.

She'd sought him out for a purpose. But thanks to his little temper tantrum, he might not ever find out what it was she'd wanted from him.

Suddenly he wanted to know—real bad.

He could still see her, walking back toward the house at a brisk clip, head down, her long braid bouncing against her back with every determined step.

"Ah, hell," he muttered as he broke into a lope, then an all-out sprint. He caught up with her just before she reached the front porch.

"Wait, Willow. I'm sorry. I overreacted."

She kept walking. "It's okay. I'm not mad. I deserved it, every word."

"No, you didn't."

She reached for the doorknob. It was locked. "Oh, perfect time for you to lock yourself out, Willow."

"Perfect time," Cal agreed, grasping her by the shoulders and turning her around to face him. "Don't run away from me. What I said, I said in anger. I'm not mad anymore."

"Hmm. You sure get over stuff quickly. I can hold a grudge for years, you know."

"Believe me, I know."

"It's not a very attractive quality."

"Not my favorite aspect of your personality," he agreed. "But you have other very nice qualities."

"Like what? You already said I'm selfish and driven and I don't care about anybody else's feelings. Certainly you don't admire *those* things about me."

"I didn't mean it when I said—"

"Oh, yes, you did. You certainly did."

"Why do you want to become a doctor?" he asked suddenly.

She stared at him, puzzled, for a moment. "Because I want to make a lot of money?"

He crossed his arms. "Bull."

She sighed. "Because I want to help people. Because I want to make a real difference in people's lives. Jeez, I sound like a contestant in a beauty pageant."

"And what are you going to specialize in?"

"Pediatrics."

"And what are you going to do once you're a pediatrician?"

"I'm going to open a clinic," she said as if by rote, because she'd said it least a thousand times, "and I'm going to provide medical care to people who can't afford it otherwise."

"Now does that sound like someone who's selfish and self-involved and doesn't care about anyone else?"

That finally earned a smile out of her. He sat next to her on the steps and she didn't run away.

"Why did you come down to the barn? What did you want to say to me?"

She shook her head. "I can't believe I was even considering it."

"Would you just tell me?"

"Everyone thinks I should give you—I mean, give us—a second chance."

Cal bit his tongue to keep from enthusiastically agreeing.

"Everyone also tells me that I'm pushing too hard, that I can't improve my memory by sheer will alone."

"I'll agree with that," he said cautiously, wondering where this was going.

"So in typical Willow fashion, I came up with a plan that would address both issues, at least in part. I was going to ask you if you wanted to be with me…for the next three weeks."

"A temporary sort of thing?" he asked, just to be sure he understood.

"It would have to be, wouldn't it? I'm moving away in three weeks. But in the back of my mind, I'm thinking, what if I don't get better? What if I can't go to med school? If I have Cal, I'll have something to fall back on—if things work out between us, if I, in my infinite wisdom, determine that a relationship with you is good for me. See what I mean? Totally selfish."

Now he got it. "So I'd be, like, your consolation prize."

She nodded, looking miserable. "It was a reprehensible plan. I'm pond scum. Because I never once stopped to consider how you would feel about it. I figured you'd take what I gave you. Just because I'm wonderful me."

"Because I'm still so pathetically nuts for you I'd agree to anything, even three lousy weeks, just to be near you?"

"That about sums up my thinking. Or lack of thinking, if you prefer that."

There was a long silence as Cal absorbed what she'd said. He watched a centipede making its way toward him on the wooden step. Rather than flick it away, he used a twig to pick it up and set it on a nearby rosebush. "You want to know what's really sad? I would have been tempted to say yes, even knowing that in three weeks you were going to dump me. I'd have just tried to change your mind, that's all. I mean, is there any reason we have to break up, just because you're going away to school? We stayed together when I went away to A&M."

"And all I could think about was when you were coming home again. I lived for your letters and phone calls. It's a wonder I made it through high school with only half my mind on it."

"But you did graduate."

"Med school is a lot more demanding than high school. With my additional…challenges…I can't afford any distractions. If I know one thing about myself, it's that I perform better if I can focus on one thing at a time. I've worked so hard for this, and I'm really afraid of blowing it."

"What if I said I'd take the three weeks and be satisfied?"

She peered at him from underneath her bangs. "Don't even tempt me."

"I *am* tempting you." He couldn't believe he was doing this. He was a masochist. That was all there was to it.

She didn't say no right away. He considered that a good sign.

"Do we even have to have a plan?" he asked. "I know it goes against your grain, but what if we just play it by ear? No promises, no commitments. When it's time for you to move to Dallas, I'll let you go."

"But will I want to let *you* go? That's what worries me. I know I'm just thinking about me again, but…see, it's a bad idea."

Cal decided he'd had about enough of this conversation. "Fine. If you want to analyze this to death, worry over every little consequence, live in the future, live in the past, live anywhere except today, you go right ahead. It's your life. But as long as you're thinking about stuff, think about this." He placed his hands on either side of her head and kissed the everlivin' daylights out of her.

She didn't kiss him back. He imagined she was too startled. He pulled away, memorizing her face, her flushed cheeks, her full lips, moist and ripe from the kiss. He'd played his last card and it lay on the table like a deuce.

"Goodbye, Willow." He released her and tried to stand. But to his surprise, she grabbed his arm and pulled him back down. Before he could even regain his balance, she threw her arms around him and belatedly returned his kiss.

Oh, Lord, her lips were soft. And she smelled so damn good, like spring flowers and…yeasty bread dough. And he wanted more than anything to tear the rubber band out of her braid and unravel her dark, silky hair and wrap himself in it. What had he done? What had he started here? If she accepted his offer, he would still lose her, and it would kill him this time.

Damn, Chandler. Now who was worrying about the future? He had Willow in his arms. What else mattered?

He kissed her until he was dizzy and out of breath. He didn't care who was watching.

Finally, Willow broke away. "I must be the stupidest woman in the world."

"For kissing me?"

"For almost letting you walk away."

Now that was what he wanted to hear.

WILLOW WAS IN IT up to her eyeballs now. Somehow she'd managed to stop kissing Cal. He'd returned to his horses and she'd returned to her hamburgers, but she fully understood what she'd agreed to. They were a couple now. They were together. And in three weeks—if they hadn't killed each other by then—whatever happened would happen. She would not worry about it. For once in her life she would live in the moment.

Anne was at her office in town later that afternoon, and Willow had agreed to watch Olivia for a few hours. Olivia was a darling little girl, with her mother's red hair and a temper to match. She seemed to particularly enjoy throwing things, the noisier the better. Willow found that a pot lid kept her busy, though. She would heave it a few feet, laugh at the colossal noise it made, then crawl after it and repeat the process. Meanwhile, Willow put together a special dessert for the last campfire, a peach cobbler. That wasn't a traditional camping dish, but she couldn't bear another night of s'mores.

The recipe wasn't one of Anne's, but rather a family favorite she'd plucked out of her grandmother's recipe box. She performed the cooking tasks almost automatically, leaving her mind free to wander where it would…which was toward thoughts of Cal, of course.

Though she couldn't go computer shopping with him, she'd agreed to come to his house and help him set up the machine. Not that she was any expert, but she could read instructions and follow them.

It was only after she took the cobbler out of the oven that she realized that, for the first time since she'd started work at the camp, she hadn't had to constantly refer to a recipe card to remind herself what to do next.

Her momentary elation was quickly dampened when she landed on the most logical explanation. She'd watched her grandmother make this dessert dozens of times. Though she'd never consciously taught herself the recipe, she'd probably absorbed the knowledge subconsciously and stored it in long-term memory. Short-term memory was the problem.

The dinner was a raging success. Wade had invited his family over—his dad and grandfather, both his brothers, their wives and assorted offspring, so the campers could get a good look at how a healthy family functioned.

Willow marveled at how different this campfire was than the first one, when most of the kids had been either hostile, scared or nonverbal. Now they teased one another in a show of good-natured camaraderie. When little Freddi expressed doubt about her chances in tomorrow's rodeo, several others jumped in to encourage her.

As the fire died to embers and the kids quieted down as fatigue overtook them, Willow sat with a sleeping Olivia in her lap. She did love kids. But it would be years before she could have any of her own. And the only man she had ever thought about having children with would have moved on with his own life.

That was if she stuck to her life plan. Before today, it had never occurred to her that she wouldn't follow that plan unerringly until she had achieved every one of her goals. But did she want to postpone being happy until then? Planning for the future was in general a good thing. But had she taken it too far? Could Cal have been right about her never having time for the present?

For a few more minutes, she practiced living in the moment, enjoying the feel of Olivia's plump, warm body relaxed against her, the smell of the campfire, the feel of the night breeze as the heat of the day gave way, and the sound of children laughing.

"Don't you have some place to go?" Anne asked, breaking into Willow's reverie.

"I can't leave you with this mess."

"Oh, yes, you can. We have plenty of helpers tonight. Go put on some lipstick and get out of here."

Willow smiled and returned Olivia to her mother's arms. "You're an angel."

"No, I'm not. I still want you back by seven tomorrow morning. Sleep or no sleep." She winked and turned away.

Willow said quick good-nights, then ran back up to the house to get her things. Anticipation ran hot in her veins as she brushed out her hair and spritzed on a bit of perfume. Hopefully the wood-smoke smell wouldn't compete.

On the drive over to Cal's house, her mind kept trying to make sense of what she was doing. Was it stupid? Was it selfish? Was she putting her future at risk? Those paths of thought were so well worn, it was hard not to go there. But each time she caught herself ruminating, she would sternly chant, "Live in the moment. Live in the moment."

She wasn't sure she knew how to live in the moment, but she was determined to try.

Willow parked in the street in front of Cal's house, then walked around to the back staircase. He must have been watching for her, because he opened the balcony doors before she even knocked.

"Hello, beautiful."

Willow took one look at him and screamed. She stepped back so quickly she almost toppled over the balcony railing. "Did you know you have a bat on your head?"

"Oh. Oops, forgot he was there. Sorry, Willow." Cal gently disengaged the small, brown rodent from his hair, then held it out to her. "Meet Frank."

She shuddered with revulsion. "H-Hello, F-Frank."

"Okay, I'll get rid of him." Cal turned and disappeared down the hallway. Taking a few deep breaths, Willow stepped inside. What else was she going to find in the *Wild Kingdom?*

Cal returned moments later. "Sorry," he said again. "October caught it last night. I took it away from him, but he'd already injured its wing."

She folded her arms. "Are there any more surprises? Orphan tarantulas in the ficus tree, perhaps?"

"There are a few more. But they stay in the attic."

"Please don't tell me you have more bats up there."

"No, not bats. Hawks. They're asleep."

Hawks. Well, that was kind of cool, she supposed. Better than bats and snakes.

"I brought you a piece of cobbler from dinner," she said, holding up a paper sack.

He looked at the sack, then at her. "Is it Nana's recipe?"

"Uh-huh. I'll put it in the fridge for later. Then you can show me the new beast."

The *beast* was a top-of-the-line PC with a lot more memory than Willow had these days, high-speed Internet capability and a flat-screen monitor. There was also a color laser printer. Cal had already set everything up in his spare bedroom. It was plugged in, humming and ready to go.

"Mmmm, it smells like Christmas in here," Willow said, admiring the shiny machines.

"Christmas?"

"Yeah. That new-plastic smell."

"What about pine trees and peppermint?"

"You have your memories, I have mine. Brand-new Barbie dolls smell just like this. It looks like you have it all together and working." She noticed some test pages he'd printed. "Guess I'll just have to go home, since there's nothing left for me to do."

Cal came up behind her and slid his arms around her waist. "No, I don't think so." He nuzzled her neck. "There are lots and lots of things you can help me with."

"Oh, really?" She was surprised by how her voice came out, all husky. The feel of his mouth on her neck, his warm breath tickling her hair, made her go warm and melty inside.

Abruptly, he released her. "Look at all this other cool stuff I bought." He opened a huge red-and-white plastic shopping bag and pulled out several colorful boxes. "You can design and print all kinds of business stationery with this one. And this is a program for home businesses. Shows you how to set up your accounts and keep everything straight for tax purposes. Oh, and look at this one. Design and maintain your own Web page. There's even a program for creating your own logo. And check this out, a digital camera. I figure I'll need to get someone to take pictures of me working with animals, to put on the Web page and the brochures. And a kit for doing your own incorporation."

"I think for some of us this *is* Christmas," she said, feeling a small thrill of excitement herself. "C'mon, let's play with your toys."

For the next two hours they took turns hunching over the keyboard, trying out the graphics program, brainstorming names for Cal's business, playing with logo designs.

At one point, Willow printed out a sample invoice. When she plucked it from the printer and showed it to Cal, she found him staring at a wall, obviously having traveled to some other place.

"Cal?" She nudged him.

He refocused his gaze on her, and this goofy, almost beatific smile overtook his face. "This is really happening, isn't it?"

"Of course it is."

"I had two more calls today. A lady in Tyler wants me to work with her daughter's show horse. He doesn't like to load into his trailer. Another guy adopted a wild

Grand Canyon burro for his kid. He didn't realize it would be completely unsocialized. I really do have something people want."

"You have something I want." Willow almost slapped her hand over her mouth. After running from Cal so hard for so long, she couldn't believe she was actually trying to seduce *him*. But suddenly he was just so incredibly sexy, with his sun-streaked hair all wild from running his fingers through it, and the way those faded-to-white jeans looked so comfortable on his skin.

Even his hands, hunting and pecking on the keyboard, looked graceful and…sexy. There just was no other word.

He grinned at her. "Could it be the peach cobbler I have in my refrigerator?"

She shook her head. "Something a little less fattening."

He held his hand out to her, and she took it. "You're right, we've done enough work for one night. Let's go raid the refrigerator. Then we'll talk about this other craving of yours."

Talk? Had she misread what was going on here? No, there was no question in her mind that he wanted her every bit as much as she wanted him. And there hadn't been any ambiguity as to what they were agreeing to. They were going to be together, in every sense of the word.

So what was this talking all about? She felt a little stab of apprehension. Was he having second thoughts about her, about having a relationship? Maybe all he really wanted was her help with his new venture.

And there she was, obsessing again, analyzing every little nuance of the situation. Why couldn't she just wait to see what he had to say?

Despite the fact Willow said she didn't want any dessert, Cal got out two bowls, cut the enormous chunk of cobbler she'd brought him in half, added a scoop of ice cream to each.

They sat cross-legged at the big square coffee table. Willow managed to eat a little.

"You look worried," Cal said. "What are you thinking?"

"That you've changed your mind."

He rolled his eyes. "Paranoid girl. You know better than that. I was just thinking, though, that we've made love exactly twice. Both times ended in disaster."

"True," she agreed.

"So I just don't want to rush it. We can take our time. We're living in the moment, right? No need to make up for lost time. We can do whatever feels right, without worrying."

She knew what felt right to her. She wanted to jump his bones this instant. But, as she was gradually learning, this wasn't just about her. Maybe Cal wanted to move more slowly. From her limited experience, he would be an atypical guy if that were the case, but it was possible.

"I'm okay with waiting, if that's what you want," she said, trying not to sound too disappointed.

"I didn't say it was what I wanted. Just throwing out the possibility that we don't have to break our necks sprinting to the bedroom."

Okay. The ball was in her court.

He scooped up the last bit of cobbler. One of his cats—October, she thought—sat patiently on the arm of a chair, watching Cal's every move just as Willow was. There was a little bit of melted ice cream in the bottom of his bowl. Cal set the bowl on the floor. The cat jumped down for his treat.

During the few seconds Cal's attention was on the cat, Willow unbuttoned the little blue cotton shirt she was wearing and shrugged it off her shoulders. When Cal returned his gaze to her, his eyes widened.

"Or, rushing is okay," he said.

She pushed herself to her feet, slung the blouse over her shoulder, and headed for the hallway. "Your bedroom's to the left?"

He scrambled to follow.

Chapter Ten

Cal's shirt was off, too, by the time he reached the bedroom door. No matter how many times he told himself that he should go slow, that he should make this time with Willow perfect, he knew it wouldn't be slow. Not when Willow was tearing off her clothes as fast as she could get them unfastened. It was dark in his bedroom, and neither of them bothered with lights. But enough ambient light filtered through the blinds that he could see her sliding her jeans down those long, long legs. Her pristine white bra and panties almost glowed.

This heat had been building since this afternoon, he realized. He'd been walking around with his jeans feeling too tight ever since, and even a discussion of Pentium chips and megahertz with a computer salesman hadn't taken the edge off.

He was really glad she didn't want to wait. They weren't supposed to be thinking about the future, but in little more than two weeks Willow might be moving to Dallas. He didn't want to waste any time, despite what he'd said.

"Here, let me." He reached behind her to unhook her bra.

"Of course." She smiled, her teeth glowing white, too. He slid his arms around her, but he kissed her long and slow before he finished undressing her.

Her hair was everywhere, hanging long and wavy all the way to her waist. He buried his hands in it, then wrapped the long strands around her, around him. It felt incredible against his skin. Comparing it to silk would be too mundane. Her hair was less of Earth, more of heaven.

"I'm glad you wore your hair down."

"I did it for you. It'll be a tangled mess."

"I'll comb out the tangles. You're not allowed to ever cut your hair." He slid her bra off her shoulders, then tumbled her back on the double bed and buried his face between her breasts. Her nipples were small and neat, dark and rosy, and hard as little marbles. He took one into his mouth and gently sucked, earning tortured little moans from her when he teased with his teeth.

Suddenly, she pushed him away.

"Willow? Did I hurt you?"

"No. Oh, no." She pushed him again, this time onto his back. She straddled him and went to work on his shirt buttons. "I just want you naked." She attacked his belt buckle with less skill than enthusiasm.

"Uh, Willow, you don't want to—oh, my." She'd unbuckled, unbuttoned, unzipped and freed his erection, which she held reverently in both hands, staring as if she'd never seen it before.

If she had any idea how turned on he was, she wouldn't play with fire. "Willow, I don't really think—" And then he didn't think anything, because his brain shorted out. She'd leaned down and taken him in her mouth.

He'd once tried to persuade Willow to pleasure him this way, when he was a stupid, insensitive college kid. Then, she had politely demurred, declaring the whole idea not to her liking and a bit icky. Now, she took to the act as if it were instinctual.

"Willow, please, you're killing me." He was ready to explode, and he hadn't even finished undressing her.

She paused only long enough to say, "Shut up and take it like a man."

"But…you'll end things before—"

"Live in the moment."

And he did. He'd known it would end fast, but he hadn't been prepared for exactly how fast. While he panted with the aftereffects of ecstasy, she just grinned at him.

"I am so angry with you," he said, though of course she knew he wasn't. "Just how are we supposed to make love now?"

"I expect we'll manage. We've got all night."

"No. I mean, you can't spend the night with me."

Her face fell. "Oh. I didn't realize— I'm being pushy, aren't I? You probably didn't mean for—"

"Oh, baby, no, that's not what I mean at all. It's just that your grandmother will worry."

"She knows I'm with you."

"Then she'll know you spent the night, that we… Come to think of it, I'd rather have her worry you were kidnapped by terrorists."

"I already told her I might not be coming home."

Cal's quickly receding pleasure turned to full-fledged

panic. "You told her that? You can't—we can't—given our history—she'll hate me."

"Oh, Cal, lighten up. We aren't kids anymore, and Nana is very modern. She was delighted, and all she said was, 'Use protection.'"

"Nana said that?"

Willow swung her slender legs to the floor and stood beside the bed to shimmy out of her panties. "I think she was something of a wild girl in her youth. So, not to belabor the point, but we've got all night."

Cal eagerly shucked the rest of her clothes. The sight of Willow, naked in the shadows of his very own bedroom with that crazy hair in a cloud all around her, had an amazing effect on him. He actually felt himself stirring, just slightly, but enough for him to know that they wouldn't need all night. Another ten minutes and he'd be raring to go.

He had a pretty good idea of what to do with those ten minutes, too.

He opened his arms. "Come lie down with me."

"Thought you'd never ask."

Willow settled in beside him, wiggling to get comfortable. It was warm, so they didn't need any blankets. She had no idea what had suddenly prompted her to do what she'd just done. She'd been kind of crazy and lustful the last time they'd made love, but not quite so…wanton. But when she'd freed his manhood from the confines of his clothes, she'd just been struck by how beautiful he was, how strong and virile. And suddenly she'd felt this flash of heat inside, like heat lightning, and she'd wanted to possess him.

It had pleased her that she could bring him so much

pleasure, make him lose control. Yet she knew he could do the same to her without breaking a sweat.

She sighed as he stroked her, his fingers performing a featherlight dance on her sensitized skin. She turned her head slightly and kissed his cheek, rough with a day's growth of beard. His eyes were closed.

"You're not going to sleep, are you?" She'd heard her girlfriends in college complain about partners who immediately conked out after reaching a climax.

He gave a low, throaty laugh. "Not on your life. Just recovering, mentally preparing for the roller-coaster ride this night is gonna be." He shifted onto one side and propped his head against his arm so he could study her. "I don't think I've ever seen you looking so beautiful."

"It's the naked thing," she quipped.

"No. It's your face. There's something glowing about you."

Willow wasn't surprised to hear that. The joyful anticipation inside her was probably oozing out her pores.

She trailed one finger over his chest, reveling in the feel of his chest hair, springy but soft. Cal was so interestingly textured—rough here, scratchy there, hard and smooth elsewhere. Everything about him fascinated her. She gently caressed his healing scar, then moved down his belly.

"You better be careful," he said when her fingers trailed even lower, dangerously close to his maleness. "You'll get me all worked up again."

"Goodness, what do you think my goal is, anyway?" She kissed him, long and hard and hot, touching him boldly in a way that felt perfectly natural to her. Amazing how quickly her body had adapted to intimacy, as if she'd been born to it, a tight flower bud that needed only a bit of sun and water to burst into full bloom.

Cal groaned, his maleness stirred with renewed interest and they were off to the races.

Once she got him started, Cal needed no further encouragement from her. He stroked and caressed in ways that surprised her, but that nonetheless had her unable to breathe enough oxygen into her lungs. Amazing that a kiss behind her earlobe could stoke the fire in her belly, or that gentle pressure behind her knee would…well, it did the same thing. It didn't matter where Cal touched or kissed or breathed or licked, it drove her wild.

When he finally moved to enter her, she almost wept with relief. But even then, he took his time, prolonging the pleasure to an almost painful degree. Almost.

Finally, finally the explosion came, rocking her to her foundations. She was sure the whole house moved, or maybe that was just a small earthquake, but her senses were blurred together in a passionate haze.

Now *this* was living in the moment.

When she got her breath back, she realized Cal had already withdrawn. He'd peaked again, but she'd been so wrapped up in her own pleasure she hadn't been aware.

Another example of her self-involvement? No, she wasn't going to blame herself just because Cal had driven her out of her mind.

She didn't feel the need to talk, and apparently neither did Cal. He pulled a sheet up over them, and she fell asleep nestled in the crook of his arm.

She didn't wake up again until just before dawn. They'd been joined during the night by both cats *and* the dog, but apparently she hadn't even noticed. All three animals were curled up a respectful distance from the humans so as not to disturb them. Willow wasn't totally surprised that Cal's animals were well-behaved even in sleep.

She knew it must be around six. She should get up, or she would be late to work. But she wanted to revel just a few more moments, locked in the security of Cal's sleepy embrace. She almost wished she hadn't slept last night, so she could have consciously enjoyed every moment.

She'd never felt like this before, never imagined how this would be. Now she wondered why she'd been such a fool all these years, avoiding Cal, wasting her energy being angry with him.

"You awake?" Cal whispered.

"Mmm-hmm. I have to get up." Her voice was laced with regret.

"Me, too. You can shower first, if you want. I relocated the snake."

"You are so, so thoughtful. Actually, though, I think I'll run back to Nana's and shower, so I can put on clean clothes."

"Does that mean you won't have breakfast with me?"

She glanced at the clock radio by the bed. It wasn't quite as late as she'd feared. "You shower. I'll put on coffee. I can have something quick, like a toaster waffle."

"Deal. I'll cook a real breakfast for you sometime, though."

"You cook?" she teased, gratified to hear there would be another time. Not that Cal was the type to make a conquest and drop a girl, but it was only natural for Willow to have a few doubts about the future, no matter how hard she tried not to.

"I'm a man of many talents."

She slid reluctantly out of bed, wishing she had time to stick around and sample a few more of those talents. She hunted around the room for her clothes. The dog woke up and stretched, watching her movements with interest. Cal watched with interest, too.

This was Willow's first morning-after experience, but she felt none of the embarrassment or regret she'd heard so much about. Last night had been just…right. No matter what the future held, she would never regret sharing herself with Cal. It was a transcendental experience.

Cal sat up and swung his legs over the side of the bed. Obviously he wasn't embarrassed, either. She tried not to stare, but he was even more gorgeous by dawn's light than he'd been in last night's romantic shadows. He stood, stretched, then headed down the hall.

By the time Willow had the coffee perking, Cal entered the kitchen wearing black jeans and a pressed chambray work shirt. His hair was damp, and the scent of soap and shampoo wafted off of him. It was all Willow could do not to grab him and drag him back to bed.

"You look nice," she commented instead.

"Jonathan told everybody to dress up for the rodeo. No holey jeans or sweaty T-shirts."

"You guys are coming?"

"It's mandatory for all the ranch employees. Jon's a big fan of his brother's camp. His stepson was one of the first campers."

"Charlie?"

Cal reached into the freezer and rummaged around,

finally locating some microwave pancakes. "Yup. The rodeo camp really helped straighten him out."

Willow managed a few bites of pancakes, which were surprisingly good. Cal poured some coffee into a travel mug for her. Then she had to scoot.

He walked her down the stairs and to her car. Mrs. Whittaker, Cal's landlady, waved to them from the front yard, where she was pruning her shrubs.

"Will the Whittakers care that you had a girl spend the night?"

Cal shrugged. "I don't know. We never talked about it."

"But you've had girls over before, I'm sure."

"Actually, no."

She had a hard time believing that, but she wouldn't accuse Cal of outright lying. Maybe he was just trying to preserve her feelings. "Okay."

"What, you think I'm some kind of playboy? Different woman every night?"

"No, that doesn't sound like you. But I don't believe you're a monk, either. It's okay. It doesn't bother me that you've had a lot more…social experience than me. I'm the one who's a bit odd in that department."

He smiled, a little secret smile.

"What's that about?" she demanded.

"Nothing. I'll see you at the rodeo, okay?"

"Okay."

He gave her a quick, hot kiss, as if he'd said goodbye to her at dawn dozens of times before. It seemed so familiar, so comfortable and so exciting all at once.

This was blowing her mind, Willow thought. But in a good way.

Nana was still in bed when Willow climbed into the

shower. But by the time she emerged with clean clothes, her hair braided in little-girl pigtails with ribbons, Nana was up boiling water for tea.

"Oh, I didn't hear you come home," Nana said pleasantly.

Willow kissed her on the cheek. "Of course you did, or you wouldn't be up so early. Thank you."

"For what?"

"For being so accepting, so noncritical. You've always been that way for me, ready with advice but never judging me. And I'm not sure I've expressed my gratitude enough."

"Well, Lord knows you got enough judgment from your parents." Nana's eyes twinkled merrily. "So, you must have had fun last night."

"I'll tell you all about it later." Well, maybe not *all* about it. "Right now, I'm running late."

CAL FELT as if he had springs on the bottom of his boots as he worked that morning. He was out on the four-wheeler, riding fences, making repairs to the barbed wire, broken rails and rotting posts as they were spotted. It was the sort of work Cal normally hated, but this morning, hot as it was, he hummed as he pounded a fence post into the dry, hard earth with a sledgehammer.

He checked his watch often, knowing that soon he would see Willow again. This was even worse than when he'd had his first crush on Willow. It had taken him weeks to get the nerve to ask her out, and he'd flown high as a kite when she'd said yes. Everyone had told him she was too young for him, but he'd persevered, knowing there was something about her that was special—and meant just for him.

He'd never stopped believing that, even when he had no hope they would ever reconcile. Now, all these years later, he was being proved right. He *had* been with other women, as Willow believed, but only a very few, and only after he and Willow had broken up. She would probably be surprised to know she was his first.

He hadn't been with anyone lately, except Willow. No other woman had given him the spark that Willow gave him. No other woman had ever made him want to be the best man he could possibly be.

After lunch, all the ranch hands, as well as Jonathan's entire family, were supposed to drive a mile up the road to Wade's place for the big rodeo. Their father and a third brother, Jeff, were both doctors and would be on hand in case of injury. So would Sherry, Jon's wife, who was Jeff's nurse at their clinic in town.

Cal's grandfather would most likely be there, too, in case any of the animals got injured.

"Are you going like that?" Jon asked him, pointing at Cal's shirt.

Cal looked down. "Oh, man." A huge stain covered the front of his shirt—probably tar from a fence post.

"C'mon inside. I got an extra shirt you can borrow."

Five minutes later, dressed in a white Western shirt with the Hardison Ranch logo embroidered on the breast, Cal headed for his truck, whistling. Since everyone else had already gone, Jon rode with him. Clementine rode in the back, leaning over the edge of the pickup bed, face to the wind.

Wade's place was packed with cars and visitors by

the time the ranch employees got there. The mood was festive, the kids running around on adrenaline highs, horses and cows snorting and pawing the ground with anticipation. The smell of barbecued beef was in the air. Pete, the Hardison brothers' tireless grandfather, was barbecuing brisket down by the pavilion. After the rodeo, there would be a huge celebratory dinner for everybody, free of charge. But donations from townspeople and parents would pour in after everyone saw what Wade was doing.

The second Cal got out of his truck, he cast around for Willow, but he didn't see her.

"Looking for someone?" Jon asked innocently. Had word already gotten around that he and Willow had reconciled? It wouldn't surprise him. They'd made out on the front porch yesterday where a zillion people could have seen them.

Cal decided there was no reason to be cagey. "Looking for Willow."

"Ah, then the rumors are true? I knew there was some reason you were in such a good mood today. Not a word of complaint when I sent you out to repair the fence."

"Sometimes the world just seems like a really good place, you know?"

"Yeah, I know."

Portable bleachers had been rented for the occasion, but they were already packed by the time Jon and Cal arrived. So they staked out a place by the arena fence. Currently one of the camp counselors was warming up the crowd with a little trick riding.

Cal still didn't see Willow. But she was probably

helping Pete, he reasoned, since meals were primarily her responsibility.

Sherry, looking cheery in her brightly colored nurse's scrubs, found them. She and Jonathan embraced briefly and shared a light kiss, and Cal saw the warm, intimate look that passed between them. A narrow ray of hope flashed through Cal every time he saw Jon and Sherry together. They'd built a wonderful life together despite their wildly different backgrounds and a host of obstacles, starting with the fact they'd lived in different cities.

Sherry turned her attention to Cal, greeting him with her usual exuberant kiss on the cheek. "How are you doing, Cal? I hear you've launched a new venture."

"Word travels fast."

"He's already got people clamoring for his services," Jon said, almost bragging, and Cal realized that what Willow had said was true. He'd included other people in his dream, and they were not only tripping all over themselves to help him, but they were sharing in his small successes. "I'll be sorry to see him leave the ranch, but I've known from the beginning that his heart wasn't really in ranching."

"Don't be replacing me too fast," Cal said. "I'm sure it'll be a while before I can make a living as a trainer."

Jon just laughed. "I've already got your replacement signed up. He starts in September."

Cal froze. He'd been afraid of this. "You're firing me?"

"What? Oh, hell no. You got a job as long as you want one. I just think you'll be leaving of your own accord a lot sooner than you think."

"Why's that?"

"'Cause you're good," Sherry interjected. "There's a need for what you do. Oh, look who's headed this way."

Cal grinned when he saw Willow walking toward them. With her girlish pigtails and wearing a pair of red overalls, she reminded him of the fourteen-year-old he'd first fallen for. Only with a few more curves.

She was scanning the crowd, and he could only hope she was looking for him. He smiled when her gaze reached him, but her answering smile was fleeting and impersonal.

He knew by now not to be surprised, but he still was.

She came closer, but instead of coming to him, she walked straight up to Jonathan and Sherry. "Hi, Jon, Sherry. It's nice to see you here. Did Cal come with you?"

"Uh…" Sherry's gaze flickered to Cal, standing all of two feet away, then back to Willow. "He's, uh…" She nodded in Cal's direction.

"Willow, I'm right here," he said, wishing there was some way he could cover up for her blunder. But it was too obvious.

Even after he'd spoken, Willow stared at him, uncomprehending, for a couple of seconds. She was studying his hair, he realized. Then his hands. "You changed shirts."

Oh. Hell, he hadn't even thought about that. "The other one got stained," he said, having no idea how to smooth over the situation.

If it had been anyone but Sherry, they might have just changed the subject. But Sherry's concern showed in every line of her face, and she was not the kind of person to turn her back on someone having any kind of trouble. "Willow, honey, are you okay?"

Willow's face turned bright pink, and Cal didn't think it had anything to do with the hot sun. Cal put his arm around her. "Willow has a little trouble recognizing faces sometimes," he said, trying not to make it sound too serious. "She saw me earlier in a blue shirt, so that's what she was looking for."

"Don't soft-pedal it," Willow finally said. "I can't recognize my own mother."

"You have prosopagnosia?" Sherry said, sounding more fascinated than horrified. "I've read about that, but I never actually met someone with it. Is it from the car accident?"

Willow nodded and pushed her bangs off her forehead.

"Come on over here out of the sun, honey. You don't look so good."

"I've had a raging headache for a couple of hours," Willow admitted as she let herself be led to a spot on the shady side of the nearby barn. Cal kept his arm around her, feeling more than embarrassment now. Willow did look a bit strange. Her eyes seemed unfocused, and her hand was clammy.

"Jon, would you get me my first-aid kid, please?" Sherry said. "I left it in the announcer's booth. And some cold water."

"What's wrong with her?" Cal asked.

"I'm guessing heat exhaustion. It's like an oven out here today."

Jon returned shortly not only with Sherry's first-aid kit, but with his brother Jeff. And Jeff did not like what he saw.

"I'm okay," Willow kept protesting. "I think I did get a little hot. I was working around the barbecue pit, and

I probably forgot to… Oh, shoot, I was supposed to get something for Pete."

"Don't worry about it," Cal said as Sherry slipped a blood-pressure cuff around Willow's arm while Jeff listened to her heart.

"But it was important…" she said, just before her eyes rolled back and she slumped over, unconscious.

Chapter Eleven

Willow was sure her head was full of cotton batting. She felt awful, as if she was going to throw up and her head were going to explode all at the same time. But she was worried about the task she'd promised to perform for Pete. Try as she might, she couldn't remember it, and that scared her worse than her physical miseries. It was something about pickles.

"Let's get her to the hospital," Sherry said.

"No," Willow protested weakly. "No, no, no, that's not necessary." She'd had enough of hospitals recently to last her a lifetime.

"Don't waste your breath arguing," Cal said. She wasn't good at deciphering facial expressions, but Cal looked scared to her.

"Honey, you had a recent head injury," Sherry said. "You need to get checked out, just to be on the safe side."

Willow knew she had the right to refuse treatment. And she was tempted, just thinking about the medical bills she'd racked up during her last hospital stay.

An ambulance was already on hand. A couple of paramedics were bringing over a gurney. Willow made a decision.

"I'll go to the hospital, but, please, no ambulance. Cal can drive me. Okay?"

Sherry looked at Jeff uncertainly. "Her vitals are strong."

A small crowd was gathering around them, a sea of bland, Pillsbury Doughboy faces. "Please," she whispered to Cal. "Can you take me?"

Cal didn't hesitate. He scooped her up into his arms. "She's okay," he told everyone. "Just a little too much heat." Sherry shoved a cold water bottle into Willow's hand and slapped a cold, wet cloth on her forehead. "Drink. And y'all take my truck. It's got killer air-conditioning and a V-8 that can outrun any cop in the county."

By the time Willow had drained the water bottle, they were well on their way to Tyler where Mother Frances Medical Center was. The air-conditioning in Sherry's snazzy little red pickup did indeed blow a blizzard.

Willow glanced at the speedometer. Cal was driving at eighty-five. "Cal, please, slow down. I'm feeling better. I probably just got dehydrated or something." Her head had been pounding so hard, the pain had probably overridden other warning signs she ordinarily would have heeded.

Cal made no reply.

"I don't really need to go to the hospital," she tried again.

"I hope you're right, but you're going anyway."

"I don't know how I'm going to pay for this," she grumbled.

"You don't have insurance?"

"Of course I have insurance. You know me better than that. I got the best insurance I could afford, which isn't a very good policy, really. The deductibles and copays are huge. Do you have any idea how much ten days in the hospital, plus brain surgery, costs? I'll be paying off my portion for years to come. I don't need to add to the debt."

"I'll help you pay it. Now stop arguing."

Willow sighed. "You don't have to pay for anything. I'm just being stupid."

"I can afford it."

"With what? Last I checked, you weren't kin to the Rockefellers."

"No, but my grandmother on my mom's side left me an old dairy farm in Lancaster. I'm renting it out right now, and it earns me a nice chunk of change. So I'm just saying, I'll help, okay?"

To Willow, that didn't exactly sound like they were living in the moment. It sounded like Cal had definite ideas about their being together in the future. A guy didn't offer to pay off medical bills for a casual girlfriend.

She didn't know whether to be pleased over his generosity or to be scared spitless. She wasn't ready for commitment. After all, they'd reconciled only twenty-four hours ago.

"Thank you," she finally said. "But maybe it won't be necessary. I'm still not sure what all the insurance company will pay for."

THE EMERGENCY ROOM at Mother Frances was blissfully empty, so Willow got attention right away. Cal sat in the waiting room, debating whether he should call Willow's parents or Clea to let them know she was here. But she'd looked and sounded much better by the time they'd taken her back to a treatment room, so he decided there was no need to worry anyone yet.

He waited…and waited and waited. About once an hour, he inquired, and he was always told the same thing—she was undergoing tests.

He was starting to get frantic by late afternoon when a nurse finally told him he could go back and see her.

He found her lying on a gurney wearing a hospital gown and looking a bit bedraggled. She had an IV in her arm, and one of her pigtails had come unraveled.

He summoned a smile. "Hey, how ya doing? It's me, Cal," he clarified, just in case.

"I'd have figured it out in a minute," she said glumly. "You're the only person to walk in here without a white jacket. Oh, my God, that was so embarrassing when I was standing two feet from you and didn't recognize you. Jon and Sherry looked at me like I was some kind of nutcase."

"I'm sure Sherry understands. She's a nurse, after all. And they won't go blabbing it to anyone." Cal pulled up a chair close to her bed. He absently went to work on her braid, unraveling it the rest of the way. Then he pulled a comb out of his pocket and started combing out the thick, glossy handful of hair.

"Mmm, that feels nice." She seemed to relax a little. "Especially after being poked and prodded and stuck with needles all afternoon."

"So, did they figure out what was wrong with you?" he asked.

She shrugged. "Dr. Patel, my neurologist, was all worried I'd had a hemorrhage or stroke or something. But they did a bunch of tests, and he said everything's okay."

Cal began braiding her hair. He'd done this for her

when they were teenagers, and the motions came back to him with ease, feeling comfortable and familiar. "I'm glad to hear that."

"He wants to keep me overnight for observation. He thinks it probably was just heat exhaustion, and nothing to do with my brain. But the headache worries him."

"Do you still have it?"

She paused before answering. "No, now that you mention it, it seems to be gone."

"I'm glad you're okay. You scared me." He finished the braid, but he didn't have anything to fasten it with. She'd lost the rubber band. "Here, hold this." He placed the end of the braid in her hand, then looked around until he located a box of rubber gloves. He plucked one of them out.

"What are you doing?"

"Just watch." He took his pocket knife and cut the end off, the part that went around the wrist. A makeshift rubber band.

"Oh, very cute. But you better hide the evidence. They'll probably charge me ten dollars for that glove."

He threw the ruined glove in the biohazard bin, then used the pseudo rubber band to fasten Willow's braid.

Suddenly, she became impatient, slapping his hand away. "What is taking so long? Why does everything take so damn long at a hospital? A room costs more than at a four-star resort, but the service you get is worse than a cheap motel."

"I'll go find out what the holdup is." He'd have done anything to make this easier for her. But he suspected there was nothing within his power to make her feel better.

He asked the ever-patient volunteer at the E.R. admitting desk, who said a room was still being prepared and it would be a few more minutes. No help at all.

When he returned to Willow's treatment room, he paused at the door. He'd always enjoyed watching her when she was unaware of his presence. He remembered back in high school, before they'd started dating, watching her from across the library or the cafeteria, thrilled by every small move she made, whether it was drinking from a carton of milk or turning the page of a book.

He didn't like what he saw now, though. Willow was studying a small scrap of paper. There were tears running down her cheeks.

He charged into the room, determined to find out what was causing her distress. Whatever was on that piece of paper, whoever had given it to her, he was going to deal with it. Vanquish the enemy.

He was a bit disconcerted when he realized the paper was a business card—*his* card, one of their previous evening's experiments.

"Willow?" he said softly. "What are you doing with that?"

She quickly brushed away her tears. "I swiped a few cards last night. I was going to get Anne's opinion. This is the one I like best. Don't you?"

The card she was studying featured a logo of a horse and a dog in silhouette, next to his name. And beneath that, the words "The Animal Analyst."

"Yeah, I like that one," he said, though for the first time in days he wasn't interested in talking about his new venture. "Willow, why were you crying?"

She reached into her purse, which sat beside her on the gurney, and produced a different card. "Although this one's good, too. The Chandler Method. Has a certain cachet."

"I've been thinking about that. It sounds good. But the fact is, calling it a 'method' implies that I could teach it to someone else. Get a whole franchise thing going."

"Wow. Franchises?"

He shook his head. "Wouldn't work. Because I can't teach it. It just…happens. I want the animal to behave a certain way, and it does. I must be employing some instinctual, nonverbal communication or body language or something. But half the time I don't know what it is."

"All right, then. We'll go with The Animal Analyst. Well, of course, that's your decision, not mine. It's your dream."

Ah. Cal thought he had an idea what was going on with her. He took the cards out of her hand and set them aside. "Scoot over."

"What? There's not room for—"

"Make room." He sat on the edge of her gurney and gathered her into his arms. "Maybe we should talk about your dream."

"You mean the one where I spend all day asking, 'You want fries with that?'"

"Willow…"

"I have to face the facts. I'm not getting better. In fact, I think I'm getting worse. I must have had a hundred people say hi to me today, and I couldn't recognize any of them. I tried to help Pete with the barbecue, but every time he asked me to do something for him, I would forget what he'd asked before I could do it. He was beginning to think I was simpleminded."

"Today was a tough day. You were under a lot of

stress. Everyone's memory gets worse when they're stressed. Like test anxiety."

"How can you say that? I was standing two feet from you and didn't know who you were. The only way I even remembered what shirt to look for is that I wrote it down in my notebook." She put her hand up to her chest. "Oh, my God, my notebook. I think I've lost it. My whole life is in there."

"It's in your purse. You put it in there on the drive over here."

"See, I don't even remember that. I can't go to medical school. I can't be a doctor. It's over."

Cal didn't know what to say. He'd tried to offer her hope in the past, but it was becoming increasingly clear that she would not be able to handle the rigors of medical school. So he just held her.

He'd seldom seen Willow cry. She'd always been so optimistic, so stoic in the face of disappointment, always ready with a new plan to get around whatever obstacle was in her path, that she seldom had to resort to hopelessness and tears.

This was, in fact, the first time he'd seen her give up, admit defeat. And it was painful to watch. It was especially excruciating given the fact that he had so recently grabbed on to his own dream, and everything was falling into place for him.

"You know," he said when her tears began to subside a little, "if there was anything I could do to fix this for you, I would."

"I know. You're good that way. And I'm sorry to be such a downer when you're all excited about your plans for the future."

"Don't worry about that. You're entitled to a good cry. This whole thing with your memory stinks. So you just kick and scream and cry all you want."

That made her laugh, just for a second. "Can I throw things?"

"You can throw things at me if it'll help. I'm pretty fast. I'll duck."

"Now why would I want to do that?"

"Because…" He debated whether to answer that one honestly, finally deciding he shouldn't hold back. "Because things are falling into my lap, as usual, and you're struggling. That's always irritated you, and I imagine it still does."

"I'm not irritated by your success," she said. "It's the one bright spot on my horizon. Because I helped, so I'm allowed to bask a little bit in the glow of your accomplishment. Right?"

"Oh, Willow." He tightened his hold on her, because he didn't want to ever let her go. "You don't have to stay out there on the edge. You can be right in this thing with me. We could be partners. I'm still just starting out, and I don't really know what I'm doing. I need you now more than ever."

"Partners?" she said in a small voice. He couldn't quite tell if she was intrigued or horrified, but he blundered on. If this was the wrong move to make, he'd soon find out.

"Fifty-fifty partners. We could have Anne draw up the papers. I'll need someone to keep me on track. You have a lot of business acumen. You could… I don't know. Handle the books and the public relations and the schedule. Keep things organized. Long-range planning."

"You probably could use someone to keep you organized so you could just focus on the animals," she said. "But me?"

"You can write everything down. Or use the computer. Might as well put that zillion gigabyte memory to good use. We'll devise systems you can work with. And I don't mean I'd just stick you in some office," he added, liking this idea more and more. "This job is going to require travel. You could come with me, help me with the training. You like animals. There are a few easy things I could teach you. And sometimes I just need an extra pair of hands."

"I don't know, Cal."

"I'm not asking you to commit to this forever," he said. "I know you. Once you get over this disappointment, you'll come up with a new dream, new goals, new plans for yourself. But in the meantime, I'll share my dream with you. I know it's not the same, but it's better than flipping hamburgers, isn't it?"

"Ugh, hamburgers. I don't ever want to *see* one again."

"There, you see? And I don't care if you don't recognize me sometimes. And the animals don't care if you forget their names or don't recognize their faces. They'll love you anyway." *And so will I.* Cal almost said the words aloud. But he figured Willow had been hit with enough drama for one day. Their relationship was still so new. And though he'd loved her forever, it might take her a while to re-learn how to love him.

"You'd really do this for me?" she asked.

"Honey, it's for me, too. I didn't want you to go away. Now I can keep you close. And I won't be striking out on this crazy venture alone."

"And what if you and me…what if we don't work out? What about the partnership then?"

"Let's just take this one day at a time."

BY THE TIME Willow was released from the hospital the next day, she was feeling a whole lot better. The doctors could find nothing at all wrong with her. She suffered no further fainting spells or disorientation. All they could theorize was that she'd gotten dehydrated—which muddled her thinking, which then escalated into heat exhaustion.

Her grandmother picked her up and brought her home. During the forty-five minute drive, she filled Nana in on her new plans to forget med school and become Cal's partner in his business.

"But aren't you upset?" Nana asked. "Not that I want you to be. But this has got to be a huge disappointment for you."

"Of course I'm upset. But I cried for about two hours yesterday, and I'm dealing with it. At least I'll have something to do with myself that's fun and interesting until I figure out what to do with my life."

"I think it sounds marvelous," Nana declared. "Cal will take care of you."

"Actually…he won't be able to pay me for a while. All the money he makes in the beginning will be plowed back into the business. And since he'll be working fewer hours at the ranch, money's going to be tight. So I was wondering…can I stay with you a few more weeks?"

"Oh, Willow, of course. Do you even need to ask?"

"I've been sponging off you all summer."

"I'm delighted to have you. There's no need for you to worry about money right now."

ABOUT A WEEK LATER, as Willow chopped up some steak for fajitas, she could hardly contain herself. It was all she could do not to get in her car and drive to the Hardison Ranch to tell Cal her good news. But he would be home in a few minutes anyway. So she applied her energy to making an extra-special dinner for him, with wine and candlelight and dessert.

She had developed a routine over the last few days. She woke up early and did chores for Nana so she wouldn't feel *too* guilty about letting her grandmother feed and house her for free. Then she headed to Cal's apartment. If he was working at the ranch, which he still did three or four days a week, she let herself in with the key he'd given her. She worked on getting his cards and stationery in order, registering his new business name, and designing ads for area newspapers. She sent out press releases to every animal-specialty magazine she could find, and when she had a few minutes, she worked on the Web site.

She also opened his mail and answered the phone. He was getting one or two inquiries a day, just from word of mouth. A few of those balked at the fee Willow quoted, but most were happy to pay up if Cal could solve their problem. She scheduled times in his appointment book. She even ran errands for him, including taking his pets to the vet and buying groceries. If he didn't have to worry about that stuff, she figured, he could really focus on his goals and become profitable that much more quickly. The sooner he had profits, the sooner he could pay her and she could think about being independent.

She also cooked dinner so it would be ready by the time he got home and showered. Over dinner, they discussed her day's activities and any new jobs she'd booked. Together, they put away leftovers and did the dishes. Then they would strategize for the next day, fall into bed exhausted—but never too exhausted to make love. She would creep back to Nana's house in the early morning.

It was the most idyllic, exciting time Willow could recall. And though she thought about medical school from time to time and she would occasionally feel tears pressing at the back of her eyes, working tirelessly on Cal's business was a terrific antidote for the blues.

She still hadn't brought herself to call UT Southwestern and tell them she wouldn't be attending. She knew she would have to soon, as well as straighten out the financial mess of her student loan. She hadn't even canceled out of the cute little garage apartment she'd picked out in Dallas. It wasn't like her to procrastinate, but performing those final steps seemed so…well, so final. So she didn't.

"Mmm, something smells good."

"I'm in the kitchen," she called out.

"I figured." Cal poked his head into the kitchen. "What in the world are you doing?"

"Fixing your favorite."

He came all the way into the kitchen, though he made no move to touch her or kiss her. He probably wouldn't, until he'd had a shower. "You don't have to do this, you know. You're my business partner, not my housekeeper."

"Hey, I like to eat too. Anyway, tonight's a special occasion."

"It is? Oh, hell, did I forget something? I know it's not your birthday."

"I'll tell you all about it after you shower."

"You're a tease, you know that? This'll be the fastest shower in history."

Willow hurried to finish up the preparations. When Cal joined her in the dining room, he froze in the doorway, staring at the linen tablecloth draped over his old scarred oak table and the cream-colored candles and ivy she'd fashioned into an impromptu centerpiece.

"You really went all out."

"Sit down before it gets cold," she admonished. She served the beef and vegetables into warm tortillas, then added grated cheddar cheese and sour cream.

Cal took a bite. "Oh, honey, this is great. Better than what they serve at Tres Rios." Tres Rios was an upscale Mexican restaurant in Mooresville that had always been one of their favorite places. All right, so Cal was laying on the praise a little thick, but he was always very appreciative of everything she did for him. "Now, spill it. What's the occasion?"

"*Texas Horse* magazine called today. They want to do a story and a big photo spread on you."

"On me? You're kidding. I mean, of course you wouldn't make up something like that. That's terrific! How did they hear about me?"

"I sent them a press release."

"You did?"

She nodded. "They want us to pick a time when they can come and watch you work. They'll send a photographer and a writer. And if it turns out really well, it'll be the cover story."

"You're kidding."

"Would you stop saying 'you're kidding'?"

"I'm just so surprised. There must be dozens of other, more established trainers they could profile. Why me?"

"Because you're unique. You're not just a trainer, you're The Animal Analyst."

Cal laughed. "You are terrific, you know that? Press releases. I never would have thought of that. You know who reads that magazine?"

"Every show horse owner in Texas," she said. "I studied their demographics."

"This could be a huge help."

"Why do you think we're celebrating?"

"I should be taking you out to dinner, not making you cook."

"You're not making me do anything. I've discovered I love cooking. In college, I never did much more than heat up a can of soup. But I seem to have a knack for it. I guess I learned from Nana through osmosis."

"Maybe you should open a restaurant. Or a catering service. Does that sound like something you'd like to do?"

A heaviness settled around Willow's heart, dampening her euphoric mood. She saw what Cal was trying to do, and she adored him for it. "It's too soon, Cal," she said, her voice thick.

"Okay. But this thing with you being my partner—I don't want you to feel like it's a noose around your neck. When you feel ready to do something for yourself, something that makes you happy, I'll support you just like you're doing for me."

"Being your partner makes me happy."

"I'm glad you're enjoying it."

Willow smiled, but she wasn't sure she liked the sound of that. Living one day at a time was hard for her. If she couldn't see a future for herself mapped out until retirement, she got a little nervous. Cal's business was her future. She'd quickly become an essential part of his achieving his goals, and she could actually see herself doing this for the long haul. It was the first time in her life she'd envisioned a future that didn't involve being a doctor, and it wasn't so horrible.

Not when Cal was part of the picture.

"Oh, you got a bunch more messages," she said. "Someone named Victor Quayles has, of all things, a pet hog named Petunia that he'd like some help with. Seems the cute little piglet his daughter brought home has turned into a two-ton monster. But his daughter is so attached he can't get rid of it. Can you work with pigs?"

Cal shrugged. "Sure, why not?"

"Cindy Lefler—you know, she owns the Miracle Café?"

Cal nodded.

"She wants to know if you can help with a cat that claws furniture."

"You don't see any claw marks on my furniture, do you?" he said smugly.

"Good point. She also wants to know how much it costs."

"A couple of hours of my time if she's willing to do a lot of the work herself. Otherwise, I'll have to bring the cat here and work with it, maybe a week or two."

Willow nodded. "Okay, I'll tell her. You also got two horse calls. One is eating his stall. The other is a hunter-

jumper named Juniper that's suddenly developed an ir-
rational fear of white fencing."

Cal raised his eyebrows. "That sounds interesting."

"I told those two you'd call them." She realized Cal
was looking at her strangely. "What?"

"Do you realize you just remembered a whole string
of messages, including first and last names of the own-
ers and the animals?"

Willow put down her fork. "I did? You're right, I did.
How odd. Well, it must be a fluke. Oh, let me get some
more tortillas. They're warming in the oven." She
jumped up from the dining room table and fled to the
kitchen, needing to be alone for just a minute or two to
process in her mind what had just transpired.

She'd remembered a whole long list of items and details. And she bet if she went into the office and checked
the message log, she would discover she hadn't forgotten a single one.

She'd seemed to be operating more efficiently this
past week. She'd spent less time picking up the phone
only to forget who she'd been about to call, or walking
into a room and forgetting why. She'd been cooking
without having to constantly check and recheck the
recipes, and she didn't consult her necklace notebook
nearly as often.

But she'd chalked it up to being in a less stressful environment than the rodeo camp had been. Working
alone in a quiet house, it was easier to remember things.
Dr. Patel had told her that stress would make her memory problems worse. Naturally, a calming environment
would improve her performance slightly. So she hadn't
given it a lot of thought.

But Cal had noticed.

"Don't go getting all excited," she muttered to herself as she pulled the warm tortillas out of the oven. It was just a fluke, as she'd said. But her heart beat a little faster.

Chapter Twelve

Willow chewed her fingernails almost to the quick waiting in Dr. Patel's office while he went over her memory performance tests. She hadn't told anyone she was coming here, not even Nana or Cal. But she needed to know whether her memory was actually improving or she was merely imagining things.

She still carried the notebook around her neck. She made notes and consulted them frequently, as always, but she found she was simply double-checking things she already remembered. Yesterday, she'd forgotten her list when she went to the grocery store. That was typical. Yet the fact she'd still remembered every single item she needed was odd.

What was even more exciting was that she'd recognized Suzy Keenes, the checker, without even glancing at her name tag.

She couldn't see what Dr. Patel was writing. His face showed no emotion—or maybe she simply couldn't decipher the expression, and her impairment was bad as ever. She really didn't know what to expect.

After a few more excruciating minutes, Dr. Patel

picked up the pile of papers he'd been studying and tapped the edges against his glossy desk to straighten the stack.

"Well, Willow, I must say, this is a surprise to me."

"Then I'm better?"

"Your scores on the short-term memory drills are fifty-six percent higher than the last time we tested, which is more than significant. What's even more remarkable is your performance on the face recognition test. You correctly identified eighteen out of twenty celebrities. That's a higher-than-normal score."

"Higher than normal for me?"

"Higher than normal for *anyone* except a hardcore *People* magazine junkie."

Willow quickly covered her mouth to hold in the shriek of joy that almost came out.

"Most of the time, prosopagnosia from head trauma is not reversible except in children," he continued. "But apparently you're young enough that your brain is still developing and changing. Either the injury repaired itself, or another part of your brain has taken over the job of face recognition. The brain is still the most mysterious organ of the human body. Have you thought about going into neurology?"

Willow let out a whoop that shook the rafters and threw her arms around the reserved doctor. "Thank you. That's the best news I've had all day—all *year*."

He more or less wiggled out of her grasp. "I'd like to use a new imaging process on you that would let me see which areas—"

"No. No more tests, no more brain scans. It's working, that's all I care about. I've got plans to make." She

picked up her purse and made good her escape before
Dr. Patel could stick any more needles in her. As she left
the office, she waved airily at the receptionist. She didn't
have the money to pay the bill, anyway. Her savings
were down to nil.

She didn't care. Her goals were back on track. She
could still become a doctor. Thank goodness she hadn't
called the school and officially withdrawn.

She couldn't wait to get back to Cottonwood and tell
everyone—Nana, her parents, Cal…

Cal. Well, that poured a bucket of cold water on her
fomenting plans for the future.

She pulled into a roadside park and shut off her car's
engine. What was she going to do about Cal?

She hadn't told him anything about her memory im-
provements. Other than two days ago, when he'd noticed—the night she'd really started to wonder if her
improved memory was more than wishful thinking—
they hadn't talked about it. In fact, she'd gone out of her
way to act a bit more scattered and dependent on her
notes and lists than she actually was. She'd told herself
she hadn't wanted to get his hopes up before she knew
for sure.

But that wasn't really true, she thought, getting out
of the car so she could pace. Just as she'd wanted strict
control over who knew of her impairment, she didn't
want anyone to know of her improvement until she was
very, very sure what she would do with her future.

And, for the first time in her life, she wasn't a hundred percent sure she wanted to be a doctor, not if it
meant giving up Cal.

Oh, hell. She hadn't planned to, but she'd fallen in

love with him all over again. Maybe she'd never stopped loving him. As her grandmother had once pointed out to her, there was a fine line between love and hate.

Willow plunked down at a picnic table. No one else was using the park; no one else was brave enough to face the late afternoon heat. This time of year, few Texans gave up their air-conditioning even for a few minutes of solitude and quiet.

The quiet wasn't really helping. The more she thought about her dilemma, the more daunting her choices looked. Her lifetime dream versus her lifetime love. She had to consider what was best for her in the long run.

"Oh, you selfish witch," she mumbled. She was not the only person her decision would affect. What about Cal? He needed her. His fledgling business needed her. Not that he wouldn't eventually get it off the ground without her, but by handling business plans and billing and scheduling and marketing, she was speeding up the process considerably.

She had taken on Cal's challenges and goals as exuberantly as if they'd been her own. And in the process, his dream had become partly hers, too. The idea of abandoning Cal now, when the venture was at such a crucial stage, was physically painful, almost as bad as when the option of med school had been snatched away from her.

She would talk to him, she decided. She would tell him everything and let him help her decide.

Oh, but she knew what he would say. He would tell her that he could survive without her, that she should carry on with her original plans. Cal wasn't needy or selfish in the least.

He might even insist.

So, no, she wouldn't tell him, she decided. Not until she'd had time to think about it some more.

She was starting to perspire, so she climbed back into her Escort and cranked up the air. Her watch told her Cal would be home soon. She didn't want to have to explain where she'd been, so she challenged the speed limit all the way back to Cottonwood.

TONIGHT, IT WAS Cal's turn to surprise Willow. He'd come home early from work, disappointed to find she wasn't at his apartment. But that was okay. At least she hadn't started dinner yet. He intended to take her out some place nice to celebrate his good news.

He'd brought home a dozen yellow roses, Willow's favorite. He was short on vases, so he put them in an old watering can and set them on the coffee table, where Willow would see them first thing when she walked in. Then he took a shower, shaved and dressed in a pair of khakis and a crisp white cotton shirt.

He heard Willow's car in the driveway just as he emerged. Perfect timing. He stepped out onto the balcony and waved at her, but she was paying him no mind. She was staring at his brand-new truck. And it was hard not to stare. It was a dark purple-gray frosty color on the upper half, fading to a true silver on bottom.

"Hey!" he called to her.

"What is this?" she asked.

"My new truck. The insurance company finally came through." He trotted down the stairs and joined her in the driveway.

She turned to kiss him, turned back toward the truck,

then did a double take. "Who are you, and what did you do with my boyfriend?"

"Ah…you are joking, right?"

"Yes. If I hadn't recognized you right away, the kiss would have done it. No one kisses like Cal Chandler. Is this really your truck?"

"Yeah. The one that got totaled was almost brand-new. Then I got a really good deal on this one. It's used, but you'd never know it." He opened the keyless entry. "Pretty slick, huh?"

"Wow, it even smells new," she said, admiring the interior. "And it's purple."

Cal cringed melodramatically. "Please. Indigo-silver frost is what they call it. It's not a sissy truck, is it?"

"Definitely not. Macho, very macho. So? Are you going to take me for a ride? What's with the fancy clothes, anyway?"

"The answer to both those questions is, we're going out to dinner. We have something to celebrate." Something more than the truck. But the rest of his news could wait.

"I'll say. I'll need to stop by Nana's and gussy up first. Can't have my boyfriend looking prettier than me." She walked around to the other side of the truck. Fortunately Cal had already stuck his keys in his pocket, so he climbed in and cranked her up. After some initial confusion with the seat belt, they were off.

Belatedly, he remembered the roses. Well, she would see them when they got back.

"You know, you could leave a few extra changes of clothes and cosmetics and things at my place."

"I wouldn't want to presume," she said primly.

"Well, then, why don't you just move in with me?

You're there all the time anyway. It would save a lot of driving back and forth."

He glanced over at her, wondering if he shouldn't have just blurted out his thoughts like that. But he'd been thinking about asking her, almost since the day she'd started working at his apartment.

She looked everywhere but at him. "Wow."

"Okay, maybe that was a little sudden."

"No, it's okay. I mean, from a practical standpoint, you're right."

"But?"

"I haven't even told my parents we're seeing each other. And I doubt Nana would have mentioned it. She wouldn't want to open that can of worms."

"You think they'll disapprove? After all this time?"

"They have memories like elephants."

"I understand." He understood that if Willow didn't want to move in with him, if she wasn't comfortable with that level of commitment, her parents' disapproval provided an easy out.

"Let me think about it, okay?" she said, worrying her lower lip with her teeth.

He reached over and took her hand. "Sure."

"Man, this truck rides smooth. It glides like a Cadillac."

Nana came out to admire the new truck while Willow changed clothes. "Now *this* is a truck!" she said, walking all the way around it. "I've never seen a pickup that color."

"What color do *you* think it is?" he asked, afraid he'd bought himself a lavender truck.

"Um, violet?"

"Indigo-silver frost," he corrected her.

"Of course, what was I thinking? Let's get out of this heat. Want something to drink, Cal?"

"No, thanks."

"Are you going to marry Willow?" She asked the question in such a light, conversational tone that Cal thought he must have misheard her at first. But he went over the words again in his mind. Yep, Clea had asked him if he was going to marry Willow.

"We've only been dating less than two weeks," he hedged.

"Yes, but you've got a cook, housekeeper, secretary and lover, all free. That sounds like a wife to me."

Cal was bowled over. He could easily imagine Willow's parents coming out with something like this. But Clea?

"Clea, Willow is a full partner in my business. She'll get fifty percent of the profits as soon as there are some. As for the other stuff, the cooking and…whatnot…she's doing it because she enjoys it, not because I'm pressuring her to do it. And anyway," he added, lowering his voice almost to a whisper, "I do want to marry her, but if I mentioned marriage now, she'd run for the hills. She has too many changes to adjust to right now. I don't want to throw anything else at her."

Clea looked down at her lap. "Forgive me, Cal. I don't know why I suddenly snapped at you. I'm just so worried about her." She cast a cautious glance toward the hallway that led to the bedrooms. "She's had to give up a lifelong dream, and that can't be easy. I'm worried that she's just thrown herself into the first distraction that came along so she won't have to think about what she's lost, that's all."

"You're partly right. She doesn't seem able to talk

about her own dreams or her own goals, even when I prod her. She says it's too soon. Meanwhile, though, I don't think it's a bad thing for her to discover there are other pursuits she can enjoy besides a medical career. I think in time she'll settle on a new career for herself. And I won't hold her back."

The sound of Willow's heels clicking against the hardwood floor put a halt to their conversation. When she appeared in a little red dress that showed her long legs to perfection, she took his breath away. She always did.

She'd taken her hair out of its braid, and it hung in shimmering ripples down her back and around her shoulders. Her feet were encased in red sandals that laced around her ankles.

"Pretty good for five minutes, huh?"

Cal tried to swallow, though his mouth had gone dry. "Excellent."

They drove all the way to Tyler to eat at Bremond's Steakhouse. It was the nicest restaurant in three counties, and the most expensive. If you had a special occasion to celebrate or you wanted to propose marriage or tell your husband you were having a baby, Bremond's was the place to do it.

"Isn't this a little extravagant?" Willow said worriedly as she studied the menu.

"No. I have money, you know."

"I know. The dairy farm in Lancaster."

"I also have some savings and investments. Wealthy grandparents on both sides, you know. So stop feeling guilty for one special night out. Anyway, we have reason to celebrate."

"It's not every day you get a fancy new truck," she agreed.

"There's that, but there's something else. I got fired today."

Willow set her wine glass down with a thunk. "You *what?*"

"This is a good thing. Let me explain. When I told Jonathan about my new business, he went ahead and hired someone to replace me. He said he figured I'd be gone by the end of the month anyway, and he didn't want to be caught shorthanded with fall coming up."

"So he *fired* you?"

"Yeah. With a month's severance pay. He figured if I could devote myself full-time to the venture, I could be up to speed in no time. He and Wade are going to put me on retainer starting in October, which will ensure at least some regular income. So as of September first, you're looking at a full-time Animal Analyst."

"Wow. That's like…walking down a tightrope without a net."

"It's not, though. Jon said if I want to come back to work for him I can, at least through October and November. He always needs extra hands then. But I won't. I'm sure I won't need to, the way things are going."

Willow gave him a trembling smile. "It's really working out for you."

"For us," he reminded her. "You're my partner, remember? Which brings us to this." He produced a thin sheaf of papers from his back pocket, slightly bent but still serviceable. He'd left them in his truck earlier, and had tucked them in his pocket when they'd arrived at the restaurant. "Anne drew this up for us. It's a partnership agreement."

"Oh."

"You don't have to read it or sign it right now. You might even want to have another attorney look it over—"

"I'm sure Anne did a fine job," Willow said hastily. "But I do want to read it." She unfolded the document and glanced at it, then tucked it into her purse. "Thank you, Cal. I know you're doing this to make sure I feel secure—"

"That's not it at all. I only took a couple of business classes in college, but one thing I remember clearly is that, when you go into business, you always protect your most valuable assets. You, my dear, are my most valuable asset. If you hadn't brainstormed with me, I never would have started this thing. And if you weren't keeping me on track, I'd still be floundering around. I couldn't have gotten this far without you, and the future would be a little dicey without you, too. That's why I'm going to start paying you a salary. It's not a fortune, but I can't keep expecting you to work for free, even with the promise of future profits."

"Oh, Cal—"

"It's the same thing I'll be paying myself. I have savings I can dip into until we're turning a profit. At first, I was leery of dipping into my savings to finance a pipe dream. But, baby, it's not a pipe dream anymore."

"I don't know what to say."

Was Cal imagining things, or was her smile just a little bit tepid? He'd thought he was offering her a safe haven, but maybe he was throwing too much at her all at once.

Well, it was done now.

WILLOW DID HER BEST to tamp down her anxiety and enjoy her salad. Without realizing it, Cal was pushing her into a decision sooner than she would have liked.

A partnership agreement? Salary? This was sounding more and more like a real job, a real commitment. He'd come to depend on her. If she made the decision to go to med school, she wouldn't even be able to give him two weeks' notice.

"I've been talking your ear off," Cal said self-consciously. "Tell me about your day. Where were you when I got home?"

"Doctor's appointment," she said, her gaze sliding away from his. The waiter chose that moment to bring their steaks. Cal waited until they were alone again.

"Is everything okay?"

"Yes. Fine, actually. It was just a follow-up visit." That wasn't really a lie, she reasoned.

"Oh. Don't scare me like that."

Willow quickly changed the subject. "Anne Hardison called earlier today. Her parents are having their annual fish fry this Friday, and we're invited. Do you want to go?"

"Sure. Those parties are always fun. Last year, Jonathan and his brother Jeff got into a fistfight over Allison."

"I guess Jeff won, huh?" Jeff and Allison had gotten married last December, as had Jonathan and Sherry. The double wedding had been the talk of the town for months.

"I don't think Jon had any serious interest in Allison. He was just goading Jeff, trying to make him jealous. It worked a little too well." He paused. "Oh, but you don't really enjoy parties that much, what with having to figure out who everybody is."

"I'm learning to cope," she said, again skirting the edges of lying. "I can't become a recluse just because I have trouble remembering names and faces." *Besides, I'm much better now. Dr. Patel says I'm close to a hundred percent.* But she couldn't make herself say it.

Just a little longer, she promised herself.

Chapter Thirteen

The Chatsworths' fish fry was in full swing by the time Cal and Willow arrived. They had discussed strategy ahead of time, so Willow could avoid awkward moments. He would stick to her side like glue, whispering names of anyone they approached or who approached them. And if Cal didn't know them or couldn't come up with a name, he would quickly introduce himself first.

Anne greeted them at the door of her parents' fancy lake house. "Oh, I was hoping you two would make it." She gave Willow a quick hug. "I'm Anne," she whispered.

"I know," Willow said a little self-consciously. "But thanks."

"I have something for you." She took Willow's hand and started to lead her into a study that was right off the foyer. But someone called to her. "Oh, shoot. Don't let me forget to show you later. Come on in, make yourself at home. Beer, soft drinks and dancing out on the patio. Fish is on the grill, boat rides a little later when it cools off."

A crowd greeted them when they entered the cavernous living room.

"Willow, good to see you up and around. You scared the heck out of us at the rodeo."

"Sherry," Cal whispered.

"Hi, Sherry," Willow said warmly, giving her a hug. "I was in good hands."

As they passed into the living room, a short, stout man in fancy Western duds approached, hand extended. "Cal. Hey, did I hear you've gone into the horse training business full-time?"

"Yeah, that's right." He shook the man's hand. It took him a few moments to come up with a name. By the time he recognized Bud Atkins, a local rancher, it was too late to whisper his name to Willow without being obvious. "Mostly horses, Bud, but I'm working with all kinds of animals, actually."

"Hi, Bud, it's good to see you again," Willow said smoothly.

Bud smiled at Willow, then returned his attention to Cal. "Hey, I got a hinky horse you should take a look at. Damn thing bites anything that moves." Bud tried to cut Cal out of the crowd as he would a steer from a herd, obviously intent on talking turkey, but Cal resisted. He didn't want to abandon Willow. "Could you give me a call tomorrow? Or Monday, whatever's convenient." He handed Bud a card. Willow had convinced him to put some in his pocket. He didn't like the idea of using a social occasion to drum up business, but he also didn't want to discourage a client like Bud who just fell into his lap. He was glad Willow had pressed the cards on him.

They wandered outside, got some cold drinks, then settled onto a porch swing. Mick and Tonya soon joined them, as well as Mick's sister, Amanda, and her fiancé,

Hudson. It would be easier for Willow to sit with a more static group, Cal reasoned, than to mix and mingle.

But she seemed to be handling everything just fine. He recalled that even at Mick's and Tonya's wedding, when she was first learning to cope with her impaired memory, she had everyone fooled. So he tried not to worry about her too much.

"This is a great song!" Tonya announced when a rollicking disco tune from the 1970s started up. "C'mon, Mick, let's dance."

Amanda grinned and stood also, trying to pull Hudson to his feet.

"No, no, no," Hudson protested. "I don't dance."

"You do now. It's aerobic exercise. Don't you want to set a good example for your patients?"

With a groan, Hudson stood. "Dirty pool, Amanda." But he smiled indulgently.

Cal couldn't help it—he envied their marital, or soon-to-be marital, bliss. He'd heard Tonya was pregnant, that that was why their wedding had been rushed. But Mick sure didn't look like a man who'd been trapped. He was gazing at Tonya as if she were his own personal goddess.

Hudson and Amanda were an even more surprising couple. Hudson, a blue-blooded millionaire heart surgeon from Boston, had given up his lucrative practice and moved to Cottonwood so he could be with Amanda.

Couples who'd struggled with incompatible careers, children from previous marriages, disapproving relatives, were all around them. Anne had given up a future partnership in a huge Dallas law firm to open her own storefront office in Cottonwood and marry Wade.

Seeing all these couples so happy gave him hope.

He stood and took Willow's hand. "Come on, let's dance."

A slow song was starting up, and Cal was grateful for the opportunity to take her into his arms and hold her tight. He wanted to stake his claim, show everyone that they were a couple.

She squeezed him tightly, and there was something almost a little desperate in the way she held him, as if she were afraid he'd slip away from her.

"Willow, honey?" he murmured in her ear.

"Yes?"

"I think I made a mistake, asking you to move in with me." He wasn't sure where the words were coming from, only that they were true and pure, and he was letting his instincts guide him.

She stiffened slightly, so he hastened to add, "Or rather, I left some things out. I don't want to just shack up out of convenience. I love you. I'm committed to you, to us. I want us to get married. And I should have just said that to begin with. But I was afraid of rushing you. I still am."

He pulled away so he could see into her eyes. They were filled with tears.

"Oh, baby, don't cry. If it's too much, too soon, just tell me. I'll back off."

"No, it's— Oh, Cal, I think I love you, too. It's just so confusing."

He pressed her head against his shoulder. "If it was easy, anybody could do it."

"Everybody does do it," she countered. "Sometimes with terrible results."

"Well, that's because they don't do it right. Granted, our track record is a little shaky. But you know what I think we need?"

"What?" she asked, slightly suspicious.

"We need to sit down and brainstorm all the elements of a perfect relationship. Then we'll work up some goals, pick some target dates, do a timeline—"

She punched him lightly on the arm. "Cal, you can't do a relationship like a business plan. It doesn't work that way. Love can't be analyzed and quantified and date/time-stamped. You are teasing, aren't you?"

He laughed. "Only half. I don't think there's anything wrong with telling each other what we both want. Even writing things down. Maybe if you saw it in black and white, you wouldn't worry so much."

She said nothing, so he just held her, savoring the fact that she hadn't thrown his marriage proposal back in his face. And she'd said she loved him—or she thought she did. He felt definitely optimistic.

WILLOW DIDN'T KNOW whether to laugh in ecstasy or burst out crying. She would suspect Cal was making her choices more and more difficult on purpose, except she knew he had no idea the choice of medical school was even on the table.

He loved her. He wanted to marry her. Could she really walk away from that?

What she had with Cal was special. She'd tried to tell herself for years that it wasn't, that it was just the intensity of her first love that made her memories so poignant, so beautiful. But she hadn't met anyone else who did to her what Cal did. And the moment she'd let him slip past

her defenses, all of her youthful love, lying dormant all
those years, had burst into life, only better than before—
more mature, more ripe, deeper, more complex.

And just like that, her decision was made. She would
not leave him. She would not go to medical school, become a doctor. For once, she was going to think about
someone besides herself. She couldn't bring herself to
hurt Cal, to toss away what he was offering her. Together,
they would make something wonderful. She would help
him become the most famous, the most successful, the
best animal trainer in the world. And they would have a
strong, beautiful relationship—or rather, marriage, she
corrected herself. All she had to do was say yes.

She would carry on with her face-blind act a bit
longer—just until it was absolutely too late to return to
medical school.

She felt instantly relieved that the decision was made.
Lighter. Happier. She could make this life work for her.
She could. Maybe she wouldn't be able to open a clinic
or find a cure for cancer. But she would have a purpose,
she would be contributing to society, and that was something she could get excited about.

"Uh-oh," Cal said. "Parent alert, two o'clock. Heading this way."

"Mine?" Willow's heart hammered against her ribs.
She swiveled around.

"Your mom, in the long white shirt and checked
pants." He was getting really good at cuing her, Willow
realized. Too bad she didn't need his help anymore.
"Your dad in the green golf shirt, just behind her."

Willow groaned. "I didn't even know they knew the
Chatsworths."

"You still haven't told them we're dating?"

"No," she said miserably.

"Well, then, let's go talk to them, get 'em used to the idea. Then it'll be easier when…if we tell them we're moving in together. Some time. In the future."

He tried to lead her in the direction her parents were heading. It looked as if they were getting themselves drinks from a cooler.

Willow resisted. "Can we just hide instead?"

"And you think I'm the one who needs to grow up?"

"Oh, okay. I just hope we don't create a scene and ruin the Chatsworths' party."

"I don't think we can top the Hardison brothers' fist-fight from last year."

Willow wasn't too sure about that. Her parents had made it pretty clear how they felt about Cal. Maybe he'd provided them with an excuse to keep her home with them another year, but that didn't mean they approved of his seducing their teenage daughter.

The terrible thing was, she was still mad at them, she realized. Cal was right. She did need to grow up and let go of the past. They were her parents, and they'd done what they'd done out of love, however misguided.

If they couldn't see their way clear to be happy that she'd found love, that she'd found an alternative to her dream career, she would just accept it and move on. They couldn't control her anymore.

She pasted on a smile. "Hi, Mom, Dad."

Marianne Marsden looked up, startled, then smiled. "Oh, I was hoping you'd be here," she said. "We decided to come at the last minute. It's such a nice evening."

Willow gave her mother a dutiful hug and a kiss on

the cheek for her father, who grunted a greeting. He wasn't much for parties.

Now came the hard part. "I'm sure you all remember Cal."

Cal stuck out his hand to Willow's father. "Mr. Marsden. Nice to see you again."

Dave Marsden stared at Cal's outstretched hand, finally taking it and giving it a quick, grudging shake. "Oh, yeah. Didn't recognize you with your clothes on."

"Dad!" Willow was horrified. She'd expected maybe a snub, not an outright attack.

To her surprise, Marianne elbowed her husband in the ribs. "Behave. Cal, it's…surprising to see you again. At one time, Willow had a Cal Chandler voodoo doll she stuck pins in."

"Mom, I did not!"

Cal just smiled. "Oh, so that's why I got that attack of appendicitis."

"So," Dave asked with a slight sneer, "are you a vet now, Cal?"

Willow could have strangled her father. He knew damn well Cal had dropped out of vet school. Or maybe he didn't. She had never vented her frustration over Cal's aborted veterinary career to anyone except Nana. Maybe her father really didn't know what Cal had been up to.

"No, sir," Cal replied affably. "I've gone into a different area of animal care. I'm a trainer. Horses, mostly, but other animals, too."

"He does a form of behavior modification," Willow supplied.

"Remember, dear?" Marianne said. "Pat Patterson told us he'd helped that little pony of theirs."

"I've become Cal's partner, actually," Willow said.

"His partner?" Dave repeated. "How can you do that and go to medical school, too?"

"Dave!" Marianne elbowed her husband in the ribs again.

"I'm not going to medical school," Willow said flatly. It was still hard to get those words out and mean them, but she was getting better at it. "It's pretty obvious my memory impairments aren't going to clear up any time soon." *Big lie.* Her conscience needled her. "I have to do something else with my life."

A loud bell ringing put a blessed end to the uncomfortable conversation. "Fish up!" That announcement came from Milton Chatsworth, Anne's father, a retired attorney and now Cottonwood's mayor. Normally staid and dignified, he always got a little crazy at his own fish fry, donning a tall chef's hat and flipping bass filets on the grill with the grace of a ballet dancer.

Several people jumped up and grabbed plates, eager to get the one of the first filets to come off the grill.

"Let's eat!" Willow suggested brightly. "I'm starved."

"I'm not a big fish fan," Marianne said, pulling a face.

"Oh, but I bet you've never tried Milton Chatsworth's grilled bass," Cal said. "It will melt in your mouth. But I think Milton will make a steak or a hamburger if you'd prefer."

"Well, I guess I could try the fish," Marianne said, and Willow relaxed. This was going to be okay. No big, embarrassing scene. Later, when they were alone, she would tell Cal that she wanted to move in with him. And marry him. She wasn't sure in what order he'd intended those two events to occur, though. Maybe he was right. Maybe they *should* sit down with pen and paper and map out a few things.

She relaxed a bit more. The idea of making concrete plans for the future always made her breathe easier.

SOMEHOW, THEY'D ended up at a table with Willow's parents. Cal felt awkward with them, but he was determined to do whatever was necessary to make peace with them. Willow was trying, too, talking animatedly about their business, prompting him to tell funny animal stories. Her mother tried to be polite, and her father didn't do much except occasionally grunt in Cal's direction. But it was a start. He would like to get along with his future in-laws.

He reminded himself not to get carried away. Willow had not agreed to anything yet. She hadn't even signed the partnership papers. She was a skittish thing, like a young filly finding her legs. She didn't like to be pushed.

But the two of them being married, having a partnership in every sense of the word, was the only choice that made any sense. Cal felt confident Willow would come to that conclusion on her own, if he just let her be.

"I'm going back for seconds," Cal announced, working his long legs free of the picnic table. "Can I get anyone anything? Willow?"

"No, thanks, I'm saving room for Deborah Chatsworth's killer brownies," Willow said. Her mother demurred also.

"You can get me another beer," Dave said gruffly.

"Sure thing." Well, that was progress. At least the

man was speaking to Cal. As he stood, Anne approached with a manila folder.

"Willow. I didn't want to forget this in all the confusion. The kids made you a get-well card, just before they all left. And I have some pictures, too, of the rodeo, since you missed the whole thing."

Cal lingered a moment, wanting to see the homemade card—or rather, see the pleasure Willow would take in it. But Dave had asked him to get him a beer, and at this delicate stage in the negotiations, he didn't want to neglect the request.

He went in search of more fish, potato salad and beer. Willow could show him the card later and take pleasure in it all over again, he reasoned.

When he returned a few minutes later with a groaning plate and two bottles of beer, Willow was still oohing and ah ing over the thick stack of pictures

"Oh, there's Mason. He looks so cute in those chaps." She flipped to the next picture. "Shannon won the blue ribbon in barrel racing?" Next picture. "Oh, that's a really nice picture of Wade. Look at that grin on his face."

Willow went on in this fashion for a few more pictures. Cal just stared, holding on to both bottles of beer. He couldn't believe what he was seeing.

"You gonna drink both those?" Dave asked irritably.

"Hmm? Oh, sorry." Cal handed the beer to Dave, his gaze never leaving Willow.

And she was looking quizzically at him now. "Cal? You look like you swallowed a june bug."

He took a long swallow of beer to avoid having to say anything. It tasted bitter to him. When he set his beer on the table, he found everyone staring at him.

"Don't let me interrupt you," he said, nodding toward the stack of photos. "Let's see the next one. Who's that, Willow?"

"It's—it's—" Understanding dawned. She stacked the pictures neatly and laid them down. "Excuse me, I have to…go…." She bolted from the table.

"What just happened?" Anne asked, bewildered.

"The pictures," Marianne said softly. "She recognized every single face."

Anne and Dave nodded in understanding. But Cal was already setting off to follow Willow. He wanted an explanation, and he wanted it now.

She walked briskly, but not fast enough that Cal had any trouble catching up with her. "Willow, come back here and talk to me."

She headed resolutely past the manicured shrubs that defined the Chatsworths' backyard. She was making for the lake, where a huge pontoon boat was docked. "Give me a few minutes, please, Cal."

"So you can figure out how to put a positive spin on the fact you've been lying to me?" He caught her by the arm and whirled her around. "How long have you been faking? Or was it a con job from the beginning?"

She looked down at her feet. "No, it was real. I started to improve a little last week. But I didn't know I was really and truly on my way to recovery until two days ago."

"Why didn't you tell me?" Cal was less angry now, more confused. He released her arm. "I would have been so happy for you."

"I know." She turned and resumed walking. He followed her all the way down the long wooden dock. She stood at the end, so close to the edge it made him nervous, staring out at the moonlit lake. The music from the party was muffled by the wind in the trees.

The breeze caught a lock of Willow's hair and draped it over her face. Cal smoothed it back for her, tucking it behind her ear. "Talk to me. Why couldn't you trust me with the truth?"

She sighed, and it sounded as if she were fighting a huge weight pressing down on her. "If I'd admitted I was better, it would have changed everything. And I liked things the way they were."

Now he got it. "Are you telling me you don't want to go to medical school?"

"I can't answer yes or no to that."

Okay, he didn't get it. "Explain."

"I've always been positive about what I wanted to do with my life. But recently, I've discovered there are other possibilities out there. Areas of my life I've been neglecting. Going to med school means giving up something else."

"We all have to make choices," he said gruffly.

"Yes, and I've made mine. I want to stay with you and be a partner in your business. I don't want to be selfish anymore. I want to honor my commitments to you and support you in your goals. But I knew a lot of people wouldn't agree with me. They would push me in another direction. I suspect you'd be one of them."

Cal was thunderstruck. She would choose him over becoming a doctor? No way. For once in her life, Willow was letting her emotions dictate her decisions, instead of her intellect. And if ever there was a time for her to use that analytical brain of hers, this was it.

"Could you still go to med school if you wanted to?"

he asked, his heart pounding so hard he thought it might knock him over. "You never called and told them you weren't going to show up, right?"

"No. I procrastinated, which is very unlike me."

"You procrastinated because you didn't want to let go of that dream. Now you don't have to."

"But I don't think I want that dream anymore."

"You don't *think* you want it. But you're not sure. If you don't find out for sure, you'll always wonder."

She took both his hands in hers, a determined look on her face. "Cal, listen to what I'm saying. No one can ever be sure they're making the right decision. But sometimes you just have to decide. Well, I'm deciding. I want you. I choose you. I love you. I want to be your partner, your wife."

Cal just stared at her, every ounce of his blood awash in pure anguish. Here was everything he ever wanted out of life standing in front of him. All he had to do was fold her into his arms, kiss her, tell her he loved her and set a date for the wedding. Here it was, within reach, a sparkling prize of a lifetime.

But did he want to be Willow's consolation prize? Did he want to live the rest of his life with her doubts and regrets? Her destiny was to be a doctor. He'd seen that in her from the time she was sixteen. Her judgment might be momentarily clouded, but sooner or later she would come to her senses and realize she could not throw that future away. Not after everything she'd been through to get where she was. Not when fate was giving her yet one more chance to realize her dreams.

What was that stupid saying? *If you love something, set it free….*

"I won't marry you, Willow. Furthermore, you're fired."

A quick succession of emotions flashed across Willow's face—shock, bewilderment, anger. She settled on anger.

"You can't fire me!" She gave him a little shove. "I'm your partner!"

"You haven't signed the partnership agreement yet, and neither have I. Gee, Willow, do you think there might have been a reason you procrastinated about that, too?"

"I was going to sign it."

"Yeah, well, now you're not going to sign it."

"You need me."

"I'll get along fine without you." That was a lie, and it took all Cal's willpower not to contradict what he'd just said and beg her to stay. He would be lost without her. "Now, why don't I take you back to Nana's? You've got some packing to do."

"I knew it. You see why I didn't tell you I was better? You're forcing me to make the decision you think I should make."

"It's the right decision. It's for your own good."

"My own— Ohhhh, you sound just like my parents when they told me I couldn't go to Stanford. Don't you think I know what's good for me?"

"Apparently not."

"Cal, you're being a complete jerk."

"I've been called worse."

"Oh, yeah? Well, give me a few moments. I bet I can come up with some real creative insults you've never heard before."

"Now you're just being childish."

"Childish? You want to see childish?" And with one mighty shove to the center of his chest, she knocked him into the lake.

By the time he sputtered to the surface, Willow was sashaying up the dock. "I will find my own ride home, thank you very much."

Cal heaved himself back onto the dock and started to give chase. But his best ostrich-skin boots were filled with water, and he had to yank them off, empty them and struggle back into them with wet socks before he could follow Willow.

By then, it was too late.

"Did you see—" Before he could even finish the question, half a dozen people pointed toward the house.

Anne stopped him at the French doors. "You can't walk into my parents' house and drip water all over their white carpet. They'll never speak to you again. Me, either, probably, if I don't stop you. Anyway, she's gone. She left with her parents about thirty seconds ago. What on earth did you do to make her so mad?"

"Not much. Just fired her and told her I wouldn't marry her."

"Is that all?"

Jeff Hardison and his wife, Allison, had wandered over and overheard the last part of this exchange. They looked at him, dripping wet, then at each other.

Jeff shook his head. "Anne, what is it about your parents' fish fries that makes people go crazy?"

Anne shrugged. "Mad fish disease?"

Chapter Fourteen

"Wow, that was brutal," said Penny Adams, one of Willow's fellow med school students, referring to the anatomy test they'd just taken. As they filed out of a cavernous lecture hall, Willow privately thought the test had been a breeze.

Willow had had no difficulties with her curriculum so far, though she'd only been in school a month. She kept busy, especially since she'd taken a part-time job in the medical library to help with her living expenses. But she found that her memory was as sharp as ever. So long as she kept up with her studying, she had no trouble with tests.

"You want to go get a coffee at Starbucks?" Penny asked.

"Sure." It was a fine afternoon in early October, still warm but with just a hint of freshness in the breeze that spoke of autumn. A perfect day.

Cottonwood's annual Autumn Daze Festival was this weekend. For the first time in years, Willow would miss it.

Willow shouldn't have had a care in the world. She

had the evening off, nothing pressing to do academically. She was moving forward on her goal chart, demonstrably closer to her dream. She had a new group of friends, a cute little garage apartment and a cat that had adopted her.

But she carried a constant heaviness in her chest.

Cal. It all boiled down to Cal.

She had accomplished some amazing feats in her life. She'd gotten into medical school despite astounding odds. Yet she seemed to remember the failures, the disasters, most clearly. And Cal was one of her disasters. She'd blown it with him not once, but twice. Three times, if she counted making love to him without even knowing his name.

She could have simply not moved to Dallas, not attended medical school. That would have shown him that she was serious about making her own decisions, that she knew her own mind better than he did. But he'd left her in such a temper, she had packed up her things the very night they'd parted, throwing clothes and shoes into boxes and suitcases as she'd tried to explain everything to Nana.

Which was exactly as Cal had intended, she realized later. He'd intentionally made her angry so she would see only one choice available.

Once she'd calmed down, she could have left med school and returned to Cottonwood. Again, once Cal saw she was serious about her choices…

Only one problem. She did not want to leave medical school. She'd realized from day one here that this was where she belonged. Reading about infectious diseases, brushing shoulders with the accomplished physicians who made up the staff here at UT South-western, had rekindled her passion for the medical profession.

She was meant to become a doctor. That was clearer than ever now. Cal was right, she'd been wrong.

But she could not deny that she was also supposed to be with Cal.

If she could just boil down the sticky dilemma to a logistical problem, her analytical brain would have seized on it and come up with a solution. But the whole Cal thing was so muddled up with emotions, she couldn't even get her brain to function when she thought about him. She would either get maudlin and cry, or she would get angry at the high-handed way he'd forced her to make a certain choice.

Penny had recruited a couple more friends to have coffee with them. They sat in cushy chairs at Starbucks, sipping lattes and frappucinos and mulling over the test that had so flummoxed everyone but Willow, apparently.

Willow leafed through a *Morning News* someone had left behind, though she was still fully involved in the conversation. She was getting better at multi-tasking.

"I still say it was dirty pool, showing autopsy photos just after lunch," Penny said. "I was so nause-ated, I had trouble telling a lung from a liver." She stole a section of newspaper from Willow and snapped it open, rattling the pages irritably.

Chad Baker peered over Penny's shoulder. "Hey, the State Fair's going on this week."

"Oh, I've never been to the fair," said Devi, a beau-tiful woman from India who was enamored with all things Texas.

"Texas has the best State Fair in the country," Chad declared proudly, as only a native Texan could. "We should go. My mom can get us free tickets."

"Well, that settles it," Penny said. "Willow, are you in? You've probably been loads of times, I guess, since you live so close."

"Actually, no, I've never been."

Chad gasped dramatically. "Then you're going. No arguments."

Willow bristled. She didn't like to be told what to do, even if the idea itself was appealing. "I really can't afford—" She stopped. Something in Penny's section of paper caught her eye. She snatched it away, staring in total disbelief.

Cal Chandler, "The Animal Analyst," will demonstrate his unique horse-training techniques.... Apparently he was going to warm up the crowd before the big auction of prize-winning steers at the livestock arena.

"Oh, my gosh, what a brilliant idea," Willow murmured.

"Great!" Penny said. She didn't realize Willow's comment had nothing to do with going to the fair.

Willow was amazed and delighted that Cal had somehow finagled his way into the State Fair. If he put on a good show—and he would—he would get loads of business off one appearance.

And he'd thought of it himself. With a pang, she realized Cal didn't need her, after all. He was pursuing his dream just fine without her, as she was pursuing hers.

She wondered if he was as lonely as she was.

LATER, AS WILLOW and her friends cleared the entrance gates to the fairgrounds, she talked them into going to watch Cal.

"Why are you so interested in this guy?" Penny wanted to know. Willow had never confided her sad romantic past to her new friends.

"He's from my hometown," Willow hedged. "Just wait 'til you see what he can do. He can take the wildest, meanest mustang you ever saw and have it following him around like a puppy dog in about ten minutes."

"And did he at any time have *you* following him around like a puppy dog?" Penny asked perceptively.

Willow's silence pretty much answered the question.

The fair's livestock arena wasn't crowded when they got there. Seating for the event was confined to two sections on one side. "Wow, look at all the jewelry," Penny breathed as they made their way through the sparse crowd, scouting out four seats together.

"And the fur," said Chad. "We're in Texas and it's not even that cold. Who needs a fur coat? Where are the animal rights activists when you need 'em?"

"Not attending a livestock auction, surely," said Devi.

Willow realized that most people in the crowd were corporate big shots and rich restaurateurs, here to bid on the prize-winning steers, which they would later barbecue. She doubted many people had come specifically to see Cal.

She hoped they would at least watch.

"There are some seats up front," Penny said, pointing.

"Oh, I don't want to—" Willow started to object, but she found herself dragged along with the crowd. She hoped Cal wouldn't spot her. He probably wouldn't, she reasoned. She'd cut off her hair recently, so that now the wavy locks barely brushed her shoulders. She certainly had no intention of approaching him or talking to him. She just wanted to see him, get her Cal fix.

At eight o'clock, an unseen announcer informed the audience that the show was about to start. Most people didn't pay attention or stop talking. Willow had this fleeting urge to stand up on her chair and tell everyone to shut up. Didn't they realize that what they were about to see was truly amazing?

Then Cal entered the sawdust-covered arena to a smattering of applause. Oh, Lord, he looked good, dressed up in his cowboy best—boots, jeans, fancy western shirt, chaps and a snowy Stetson that emphasized his burnished tan.

Penny issued a low whistle. "Oh, man. Don't tell me you let that one get away."

"'Fraid so," Willow said glumly. Looking at him, watching him move, didn't just make her heart ache. Her whole body hurt.

"Who dumped who?" Penny wanted to know.

"I guess technically he dumped me. Although, come to think of it, I was the one who pushed him in the lake. I was ready to give up med school to stay with him, but he wouldn't let me do it. He said I'd regret it."

"Was he right?"

"Yes," Willow answered in a small voice. "But sometimes I wish I could live two lives at the same time."

"My boyfriend lives in Boston," Penny groused. "He works for the Red Sox. I applied to med schools up there, but…" She shrugged. "Here I am."

"But you've stayed together?"

"Yeah. That's what unlimited cell phone minutes are for." She looked a little glum, though.

Cal began talking into a wireless mike attached to his shirt. His introduction was obviously memorized and a little stilted, Willow thought. Few people were paying attention. But as he warmed to his subject, he strayed from his rehearsed comments and loosened up a bit. The crowd got a little quieter.

"But y'all aren't here to hear me talk," he said. "Let's bring out my first patient. I've never met this horse you're about to see. In fact, less than forty-eight hours ago, he was running free on the plains of Montana. I don't know how old he is, but he's probably never had contact with humans until now."

A high-pitched horse squeal punctuated Cal's sentence. Then some snorting and the unmistakable sound of a horse trying to kick down a stall.

Penny reflexively grabbed Willow's knee and squeezed. Just as Willow spotted where the horse was penned up, the gate opened, and a couple of tons of furious wild horse burst into the arena, neighing and bucking and spinning like a tornado. Then he broke into a fast gallop, nearly running headlong into a fence before skidding to a stop, turning and galloping again.

Every eye in the crowd was watching now. No one said a word.

Cal just stood in the center of the arena, his hat in one hand now. "Cyclone here hasn't seen too many fences in his day," Cal said, sounding not the least bit intimidated by the fact that he could be kicked to death any moment. "His instinct is to run as far and as fast as he can from what he perceives as threats to his life, and the barriers are frustrating him. My first job is to show him I'm not a threat. So I just stand here real still until he gets curious about me."

Willow compared Cal's performance to the first time she watched him, when he was working with the old plug Danny. Then, he'd pretty much ignored his audience. Now he was playing to them like a natural showman. She wouldn't have guessed his public speaking skills were so strong.

Had someone coached him? she wondered, a surge of jealousy coursing through her. *She* should have been the one to help him prepare for this big moment.

The horse continued to run. Cal kept up an interesting patter until the horse slowed. Then, just as predicted, it started watching Cal, obviously curious.

The first time it approached, Cal waved his hat in the horse's face and it skittered away—just as he'd done with the Shetland pony, Pepper. "I'm letting him know that I'm not ready to play yet. I want to communicate to this horse that, while I won't hurt him, I'm also the boss. Horses are big on hierarchy. If I let him establish dominance, I'm doomed."

"This is so interesting," Penny whispered. "He's kind of like that horse whisperer guy."

"He uses some of the same techniques," Willow whispered back. "But a lot of what he does is uniquely Cal."

After a few more rebuffs, Cal allowed the mustang to stand near him. The horse's head was down, his ears forward. He seemed to be waiting for some sign of acceptance. Cal offered him a carrot. The horse meekly accepted it, but he jerked away when Cal tried to stroke his neck. Cal turned his back on the horse and walked away. In moments, the horse followed him—trotting after him like a puppy, just as Willow had predicted.

A few more minutes of this back and forth, and Cal had nylon halter and a lead rope on the horse.

"I don't have time tonight to actually ride him," Cal said. "That would take a few hours."

A collective gasp rose from the crowd. These were horse people; they knew how long it took to break a completely wild horse by traditional methods. Weeks, not hours.

"I know y'all are anxious to get to the auction, so me and Cyclone'll be on our way. But my business card is attached to the auction program if any of you want to talk—" He stopped, and Willow realized he was staring squarely at her. For a few moments he was struck silent, and a look of sadness came over his face. The horse, who only a few minutes ago would have loved to kick Cal's head off, seemed to feel the sadness. He nuzzled Cal's cheek and gave a low, soft whinny.

"He's looking at you," Penny whispered.

The crowd didn't know exactly what was going on, but they sensed it on some level. The silence was deafening.

Finally, Cal looked away. "Uh, anyway, if you want to talk, give me a call. Good night, and good luck with your bidding."

The applause thundered across the arena. Cal, his grip firm on the mustang's lead rope, leaned in and whispered something to him. The horse's ears twitched and his matted tail swished, but that was the only indication that the applause bothered him.

As Cal disappeared through a gate with one final

wave, Willow knew that merely seeing him wasn't going to be enough. She had to talk to him, tell him what a great job he'd done, what a brilliant idea this was. He was bound to be deluged with calls.

And she needed to thank him.

"I have to go find him," she said, standing up.

"You go, girl," Penny said with a double thumbs-up. "Don't let him get away again."

Willow worked her way through the crowd, then wandered around until she found a way down to the arena floor level. She had to duck through one No Admittance gate, then sweet-talk her way past a security guard, but she finally located the animal pens. Lots of 4-H and Future Farmers kids were hanging out with their prize-winning animals. Lots of sad faces—they would be saying goodbye soon.

She didn't need to ask where Cal was. She just followed the excited voices and found the area where the most people were congregated. A large, heavily fortified pen had been set up for the mustang stallion. Several people, mostly kids, were gathered around, some standing on the metal fencing to see over.

Willow worked her way up to the fence. Cal was inside the pen with the horse, which looked much bigger this close up. The horse was placidly munching hay. Cal was gently brushing the horse's mud-speckled neck. His lips were moving, so she knew he was talking to the animal as only he could. His attention was one hundred percent on the horse. He was in a zone, what she jokingly called his "animal zone," where he tuned out everything but his communication with whatever beast he was working on.

She knew, too, that the horse was listening. One ear was rotated backward, pointing directly at Cal.

Willow moved around the pen until she was in his line of sight. She stepped up onto the first rail of the fence, but she didn't say anything. She knew he didn't like to be interrupted when he was this tightly bonded with one of his animals. She contented herself with watching him, drinking in the sight of him, the tenderness in his face, the gentle way he touched the wild horse.

Suddenly, he saw her. He jumped, startled out of his semi-trance. "Willow?"

The horse reacted, too. The moment Cal took his total attention off the mustang, it wheeled around faster than the eye could follow and kicked Cal right in the head. With a surprised look, Cal crumpled to the ground.

Chapter Fifteen

Several people screamed as Cal hit the sawdust. Then everyone was talking at once. Willow just stared in horror, knowing this was all her fault. She shouldn't have distracted Cal when he was penned up with a dangerous animal.

No one was rushing in to Cal's aid.

"Get the paramedics!" someone shouted.

"I doubt the paramedics will go into that pen with that horse," someone else said.

"Oh, for heaven's sake!" Willow climbed the rest of the way over the fence and into the pen. The wild horse snorted and pawed the ground threateningly, but Willow was far more scared for Cal than she was about the horse. She pointed her finger at it. "You just back off, buster!"

This seemed to work. The horse did back off a couple of steps, though he kept his bewildered gaze on Willow.

She knelt down by Cal's side. He was unconscious but breathing. She felt his carotid artery, which pulsed with reassuring strength.

She needed to get him out of the pen. She was trying to figure out where to grab on to him when his eyes fluttered open.

"Oh, Cal, thank God."

"What happened?" He rolled onto his side and pushed himself up.

"Easy. Take it slow. Your new best buddy kicked you in the head." She was not a doctor yet, but she saw no sign of injury other than the bruise forming at Cal's temple.

He stared at Willow with bleary eyes. "Who are you?"

Willow's heart just about stopped. "I'm Willow."

"No, you're not. Willow has really long hair, hangs all the way to her butt."

"I cut it," she said almost desperately. Now she had an inkling of how Cal had felt when she didn't recognize him, and it wasn't pleasant. "I didn't have time to mess with it. And I thought cutting it would make me look more mature."

He shook his head. "I told Willow in no uncertain terms that she was not allowed to cut her hair."

"All right. I cut my hair because I was mad at you. I needed an outward sign of my independence from you."

He just stared at her, uncomprehending.

Two paramedics in white had arrived. The crowd made room for one of them to approach the fence. "Sir?"

Cal waved and flashed a loopy smile. "Hi."

The man looked at Willow. "Can you get him out of there?"

She stood up and offered her hand to Cal. "Can you stand up?"

He did, with some difficulty. "Wow, can you stop everything from spinning around?"

She put an arm around his waist and let him lean on her. "C'mon, Cal, let's move." Slowly they progressed to the gate, where someone opened it just wide enough that they could slip out. She breathed a sign of relief at escaping the horse, which could have turned them both into mincemeat at any time.

The paramedics took over. They got him onto a stretcher, despite his weak protests that he was okay.

"Was he unconscious at any time?" the paramedic asked.

"Yes. And he's disoriented. He doesn't recognize me, and I'm his girlfriend. Um, ex-girlfriend."

The paramedic frowned. "Let's roll."

"Can I go with you?" Willow asked desperately. "I'm in med school." She didn't add that she'd had exactly five weeks of medical education to date.

The paramedic rolled his eyes. "Yeah, come on.

After they loaded Cal's stretcher onto the ambulance, Willow climbed in herself. The paramedic who stayed in the back to treat Cal had a quick consultation by phone with a doctor, then started an IV and put a cold pack on Cal's head.

"Cal?" Willow said, touching his arm.

"Hmm? Oh, it's you. The one who's not Willow."

The paramedic exchanged a worried glance with Willow.

"Willow's going to be a doctor," Cal informed them.

"Yes, I know," Willow said softly.

"I'm still in love with her. Did you know that?"

Tears sprang into Willow's eyes. Her throat felt thick. She couldn't answer.

"I sent her away. Kind of like the way I sent that mustang away. He was curious, but he wasn't ready to bond. I had to send him away for his own good."

"Willow's not a horse," Willow managed. "And she wasn't just curious. She was in love with you, too."

"Maybe she was," Cal said. "But I couldn't let her turn her back on her dream, could I? Not after a twist of fate took it away, then another one gave it back? I know what it's like to chase after a dream. It's almost the best feeling in the world. If a person is lucky enough to have a dream and the means to go after it, they're almost obligated to do so, don't you think?"

Willow nodded, though she wasn't sure Cal could see her. His head was immobilized in a cervical collar, his face pointing straight up at the ceiling.

"Don't you think people ought to become the best people they can be, so they can give the world everything possible?"

"Yes, I do believe that."

"If Willow had given up her dream to help me achieve mine, I'd be cheating her of something important. And it might have stood between us forever. She might have even started to resent me."

Willow didn't agree out loud. But she'd come to the same conclusion herself.

"Do you want to know the worst thing?"

She nodded, not sure whether he could even see her.

"I wanted to be selfish. I wanted to keep her all to myself and let her give it all up. I was so close to doing just that."

"But you didn't."

"No, I hurt her instead. I didn't enjoy it, and I feel guilty about it every day."

"She's coping," Willow said.

"If I tell you a secret, you promise not to tell Willow?"

The paramedic raised his eyebrows at this. He was listening intently.

"I won't breathe a word to her," Willow promised. She wouldn't have to.

"I own this old dairy farm in Lancaster. You know where Lancaster is?"

"Yes." She remembered that he'd told her about the farm his grandmother had left him, that he was leasing out the land for grazing.

"I'm spending every spare minute I have to fix up the old place. It's got an old farmhouse on it, and barns and paddocks. It'll make a great training facility. Instead of traveling all over, I can sit back and let the animals come to me."

That's a great idea! And he would be close, so close. Lancaster was maybe a thirty-minute drive from her apartment in East Dallas. Willow's heart pounded with excitement.

"I figure by Christmas, the place'll be livable. I'm going to ask Willow to marry me then. Not like I did before—that was awful, asking her to shack up with me and then saying that maybe, someday, we could get married. No wonder she didn't jump at the chance. Talk about wishy-washy."

Willow was the one who'd been stupidly wishy-washy, but she decided not to point that out. She couldn't have talked, anyway. Her throat was clogged with tears. Tears were streaming down her face. She sniffled loudly.

"I'm gonna get a ring and get down on one knee and

everything. See, she could live at the farm and still commute to school. It's a bit of a drive, but she could quit her part-time job if that would help."

She wondered how he knew she *had* a part-time job. Had he been checking up on her? Of course he had. Nana would have filled him in on every detail, if he'd acted interested.

"That way, we could both chase after our dreams. 'Cause you know what? Dreams are a lot more fun when you can share them with someone else. I've been lonely without Willow's support and encouragement."

"Yeah, I know what you mean. But why wait? Why don't you ask Willow to marry you now?"

"'Cause I want the farm to look better before I show it to her," he admitted.

"Willow has a great imagination. She'll see the potential."

"You think?"

She unfastened her seat belt and moved to stand over Cal, so he could see her. "Willow will say yes. I guarantee it."

Just then the ambulance made a violent sway and Willow fell practically on top of Cal. The paramedic cleared his throat in disapproval and Willow tried to get herself upright. But she found Cal's arms holding her prisoner.

"Hi, Willow," he said, just before he kissed her.

"I can't allow you—excuse me," the paramedic tried, but Cal ignored him.

Willow indulged in the kiss for only a few seconds. What if she sent Cal's blood pressure soaring and he hemorrhaged? She, if anyone, knew that brain injuries weren't something to trifle with. She pulled away.

"You wicked, wicked man. You knew it was me all along."

"Not the first fifteen or twenty seconds. You cut your hair. Had me all confused."

She glared at him. "You wretched faker."

"Hey, turnabout's fair play."

She couldn't really argue that one. And she didn't get the opportunity. They'd arrived at the hospital, and Cal's stretcher was whisked out of the ambulance and into the E.R. of Baylor Medical Center.

CAL GRINNED so much during the various tests the doctors administered that they were convinced he'd addled his brains. No needle pricks bothered him. No dire warnings about concussions and slipping into a coma fazed him. In the end, his tests came out normal and the doctors declared he had nothing but a mild concussion, for which they told him to take some Tylenol. Of course, they thought he was crazy, but that didn't bother him.

He was still grinning when he emerged into the E.R. waiting room to find Willow pacing. He paused before announcing his presence just so he could gaze at her. He'd probably still give her a hard time about the haircut, but it actually looked good on her. Made her look less like a college kid and more like the grown-up woman she'd become.

He didn't make a sound, but she looked over and saw him anyway.

"Cal!" She nearly tripped over a toddler in her haste to get to him. She threw her arms around him and almost knocked him over. "I've been so worried. What took so long?"

"You know hospitals. Everything takes forever. I'm fine. Just a little concussion."

"Concussion?"

Her expression of intense worry almost made Cal laugh. "I'm fine," he repeated. "Hardly even a headache. Want to go shopping?"

"Shopping? It's after midnight."

"You don't think we can find an all-night jewelry store? Because someone assured me you would say yes if I asked you to marry me."

"And someone assured me he would do it up right this time." She looked around and winced. "Not in a hospital waiting room, please."

They went outside into the warm, clear night. "You'll stay with me tonight, of course," Willow said practically. "My apartment is only a five-minute cab ride from here. Since you have a concussion, someone will need to wake you up periodically during the night."

"You're sounding like a doctor already." He threw an arm around her shoulders. "How about if we just stay up all night and talk about our future? We need some new goal charts, I think, and a time line for when we'll have children and how we'll save money for their college education— Oh, wait a minute, I'm doing it all wrong again." He dropped to one knee right there on the walkway. "Will you marry me, Willow? I'm afraid this is as proper as I'm going to get."

She started laughing and crying all at the same time. She couldn't get any words out, but she nodded. And suddenly the breeze felt a little fresher, the stars a little brighter and his future a lot sunnier.

WINTER FINALLY arrived in Lancaster, Texas, just in time for Christmas. Balmy days and cool nights had abruptly given way to a whistling north wind and snow flurries.

Willow, exhausted from her end-of-term exams, was nonetheless excited about the upcoming holiday, her first Christmas as a married woman.

Though Willow's parents had wanted to give her a big wedding with all the trimmings, Willow hadn't felt she could spare the time to plan it—and she hadn't wanted to wait, anyway. Cal, impatient to move ahead with the next phase of their lives, had wanted to elope to Vegas.

They'd compromised with a small church ceremony just before Thanksgiving. Their abbreviated honeymoon had consisted of a weekend trip to Texas's South Padre Island. Then they'd moved their things into the cavernous farmhouse in Lancaster, which Cal had been working on every weekend.

The house still had a long way to go, but its former grace and charm were starting to shine through the years of grime and neglect. At least the roof didn't leak anymore, and they now had an oven that worked well enough that they could roast a turkey. Paint and plaster did wonders for the appearance and kept the place cleaner. The dull oak floors had been almost magically transformed with some sanding, staining and polyurethane.

Willow had found several huge rolls of red velvet ribbon in a bargain bin at a thrift store. She fashioned it into bows, which she stuck everywhere, including all over the Christmas tree, and supplemented the décor with evergreen branches and pine cones dusted with silver glitter. Her decorations wouldn't pass muster with Martha Stewart, but they were warm and cheerful. All three cats dashed around the house as if it were their personal playground, pouncing on pine cones and batting them under the furniture.

The scent of roasting turkey and cornbread dressing wafted through the house. A huge plank table in the dining room, which was just too big for them to use when they were alone, was set with holly-decorated linens and the Christmas china she'd collected as a girl but never had occasion to use.

At ten o'clock, the doorbell rang. Nana and Willow's parents stood on the wide front porch, their arms loaded with packages, wool mufflers wrapped around their necks against the cold. Willow greeted them with hugs and kisses and immediately offered them coffee, tea and hot chocolate to drink.

"We don't have central heating yet," she explained. "Near the fire it's warm, though. And in the kitchen."

Nana, of course, made a beeline for the kitchen. She'd brought some homemade pies, but she was still itching to cook, and Cal, who had taken charge of the feast, accommodated her.

Cal's parents and grandfather arrived a few minutes later, followed immediately by his older sister, Denise, and her husband, Tom, who'd driven down from Michigan.

Soon the house was filled with voices and laughter. Willow had a warm glow inside her that had nothing to do with her hot chocolate. This was how holidays should feel. She remembered Christmases like this from her childhood, when her grandfather was still alive, and her aunts and uncles and cousins would all gather at someone's house and eat and drink and laugh and watch football and eat some more.

When the turkey was finally cooked and they all gathered around the festive table, Nana and Doc Chandler both said a short blessing. Then Nana commented, "This is just like a Norman Rockwell painting."

"Only one thing missing, though," Doc said. "The patter of little feet." He looked straight at Willow when he said it.

Did he know? Could he tell just by looking at her? Oh, Lord, she hadn't even told Cal yet! She'd only taken the test yesterday, and she wanted to get a doctor's opinion before she told anyone.

"Um, excuse me," she said, getting up quickly from the table before her face gave her away. "I forgot the, uh, croutons…." She walked briskly toward the kitchen, resisting the urge to run.

But she didn't fool Cal for a minute. She should have known he would figure out something was up. He was an expert at reading an animal's body language, but she'd discovered he was pretty darn good at reading hers, too.

She leaned against the edge of the sink, breathing slowly, trying to regain her composure. Cal came up behind her.

"Croutons? For what, the cranberry sauce? There's no salad on the table."

She turned around and found herself in the circle of his arms. "I misspoke."

His eyes danced. "Are you pregnant?"

She caught her bottom lip in her teeth. "Think so."

Cal whooped and spun her around.

"No, don't, don't, you'll make me throw up if I get dizzy. Look, I know this doesn't exactly fit neatly into our goals—"

"We'll make new goal charts."

"Do you think I can still manage school?"

"Oh, honey, of course. I'll be here. I'll take care of the baby. We'll make it work just like we've made everything else work. We'll come up with a plan."

Nana peeked into the kitchen. "Everything all right in here?"

"We're having a baby," Cal said.

"What?" said Dave Marsden. "A baby? I'm gonna be a grandfather?" And pretty soon everybody was in the kitchen, letting their food get cold while they hugged Willow and thumped Cal on the back as if he'd done something heroic and stupendous.

It wasn't heroic, Willow decided. It was miraculous. Fate's way of forcing her hand once again. Yet she didn't resent the change of plans one bit. There seemed to be a method to the madness that occasionally visited her life. If she hadn't had the car accident, she probably never would have let her guard down long enough to get back together with Cal. And while having a baby a few years earlier than she'd planned might *seem* like a problem, Willow knew it was truly a blessing, yet another in a life that seemed to be overflowing with blessings these days.

She and Cal wore matching, goofy grins the rest of the day.

* * * * *

Look for Kara Lennox's upcoming miniseries,
BLOND JUSTICE, *beginning in May 2005,*
only from Harlequin American Romance.

Turn the page for excerpts
from next month's four lively and delightful books
from American Romance!

Archer's Angels by Tina Leonard
(American Romance #1053)

Archer Jefferson—he's brother number eight in Tina's COWBOYS BY THE DOZEN miniseries. Enjoy this popular author's high-energy writing, quirky characters and outrageous situations. And in June, come back for more with *Belonging to Bandera*!
Available in February 2005.

Clove Penmire looked around as she got off the bus in Lonely Hearts Station, Texas. For all her fascination with cowboys and the lure of the dusty state she'd read so much about, she had to admit that small-town Texas was nothing like her homeland of Australia.

A horse broke free from the barn across the street, walking itself nonchalantly between the two sides of the old-time town. A cowboy sprinted out of the barn and ran after his horse, but he was laughing as he caught up to it.

Clove smiled. From the back she couldn't tell if the man was handsome, but he was dressed in Wranglers and a hat, and as far as she could tell, this cowboy was the real thing.

And she had traveled to Texas for the *real thing*.

That sentiment would have sounded preposterous, even to Clove, just a month ago. Until she'd learned that her sister, Lucy, couldn't have a baby. Of course, people all over the world couldn't always conceive when they wanted to. They adopted or pursued other means of happiness. She hadn't been too worried— until Lucy had confessed that she thought her husband might leave her for a woman who could bear children.

Clove's thoughts then took a decidedly new trajectory, one that included fantasies of tossing her brother-in-law into the ocean.

Now the cowboy caught her interested gaze, holding it for just a second before he looked back at his horse. The man was extremely handsome. Breathtakingly so. Not the cowboy for her, considering her mission, and the fact that she was what people politely referred to as…a girl with a good personality.

She sighed. If Lucy had gotten all the beauty, their mother always said with a gentle smile, then Clove had gotten all the bravery. Which was likely how she'd ended up as a stuntwoman.

She watched the cowboy brush his horse's back with one hand, and fan a fly away from its lovely flame-marked face. He was still talking to it; she could hear low murmuring that sounded very sexy, especially since she'd never heard a man murmur in a husky voice to *her.*

"Archer Jefferson!" someone yelled from inside the barn. "Get that cotton-pickin', apple-stealin', dog-faced Appaloosa in here!"

"Insult the man, but not the sexy beast!" he yelled back.

Clove gasped. Archer Jefferson! The man she'd traveled several time zones to see! Her Texas Archer of two years' worth of e-mail correspondence!

He was all cowboy, more cowboy than she'd come mentally prepared to corral. "Whoa," she murmured to herself.

Okay, a man that drool-worthy did not lack female friends. Why had he spent two years writing to a woman he'd never meet? She wrinkled her nose, pushed her thick glasses up on her nose and studied him further. Tight jeans, dirty boots. Long, black hair under a black felt hat—he'd never mentioned long hair in their correspondence. Deep voice. Piercing blue eyes, she noted as he turned around, catching her still staring at him. She jumped, he laughed and then he tipped his hat to her as he swung up onto the "dog-faced" Appaloosa, riding it into the barn in a manner the stuntwoman in her appreciated.

Just how difficult would it be to entice that cowboy into her bed? Archer had put ideas about his virility in her mind, with his Texas-sized bragging about his manliness and the babies popping out all over Malfunction Junction ranch.

Seeing him, however, made her think that perhaps he hadn't been bragging as much as stating fact. Her heart beat faster. He'd said he wasn't in the relationship market.

But a baby, just *one* baby…

Her Secret Valentine by Cathy Gillen Thacker
(American Romance #1054)

This is the entertaining and emotional fifth installment
in Cathy's series, THE BRIDES OF HOLLY SPRINGS.
With a little help from Cupid—and the close-knit Hart
clan—a long-distance couple has a Valentine's Day re-
union they'll never forget! You'll be captivated by
Cathy's trademark charm, but you'll also identify with
the real issues explored in this book—the tough choices
faced by a two-career couple in today's world.
Available in February 2005.

"How long is this situation between you and Ashley
going to go on?" Mac Hart asked.

Cal tensed. He thought he'd been invited over to his
brother Mac's house to watch playoff football with the
rest of the men in the family. Now, suddenly, it was
looking more like an intervention. He leaned forward
to help himself to some of the nachos on the coffee
table in front of the sofa. "I don't know what you mean."

"Then let us spell it out for you," Cal's brother-in-law,
Thad Lantz, said with his usual coachlike efficiency.

Joe continued. "She missed Janey's wedding to Thad

in August, as well as Fletcher's marriage to Lily in October, and Dylan and Hannah's wedding in November."

Cal bristled. They all knew Ashley was busy completing her OB/GYN fellowship in Honolulu. "She wanted to be here but since the flight from Honolulu to Raleigh is at least twelve hours, it's too far to go for a weekend trip. Not that she has many full weekends off in any case." Nor did he. Hence, their habit of rendezvousing in San Francisco, since it was a six- or seven-hour flight for each of them.

More skeptical looks. "She didn't make it back to Carolina for Thanksgiving or Christmas or New Year's this year, either," Dylan observed.

Cal shrugged and centered his attention on the TV, where a lot of pregame nonsense was taking place. "She had to work all three holidays." He wished the game would hurry up and start. Because the sooner it did, the sooner this conversation would be over.

"'Had to,' or volunteered?" Fletcher murmured with a questioning lift of his dark eyebrows.

Uneasiness settled on Cal. He'd had many of the same questions himself. Still, Ashley was his wife, and he felt honor-bound to defend her. "I saw her in November in San Francisco. We celebrated all our holidays then." In one passion-filled weekend that had, oddly enough, left him feeling lonelier and more uncertain of their union than ever.

Concerned looks were exchanged all around. Cal knew the guys in the family all felt sorry for him, which just made the situation worse.

Dylan dipped a tortilla chip into the chili-cheese sauce. "So when's Ashley coming home?" he asked curiously.

That was just it—Cal didn't know. Ashley didn't want to talk about it. "Soon," he fibbed.

All eyes turned to him. Cal waited expectantly, knowing from the silence that there was more. Finally, Joe cleared his throat. "The women in the family are all upset. You've been married nearly three years now, and most of that time you and Ashley have been living apart."

"So?" Cal prodded.

"So, they're tired of seeing you unhappy." Dylan took over where Cal had left off. "They're giving you and Ashley till Valentine's Day—"

Their wedding anniversary.

"—to make things right."

"And if that doesn't happen?" Cal demanded.

Fletcher scowled. "Then the women in the family are stepping in."

"Damn, here she comes again."

Third time this week that Erika Dunn had shown up
uninvited at his ranch house. She was making it difficult
for Judd to settle into his self-imposed role as a recluse.

Judd Foster peered through the dusty slats of the mi-
niblinds and heavy, outdated drapes that covered his
living room window. She had the kind of unadvertised
and understated beauty that intrigued a man who'd been
trained to look beyond surface appearances. The woman
didn't just *walk* to his house; she practically floated. She
was too vibrant, too energized. He didn't want her coming around, spreading good cheer and flashing that infectious smile.

He just wanted to be left alone.

His attention shifted to the covered dish in her hand. Judd's mouth watered involuntarily. He wondered what delicious culinary temptation she had delivered this time. More of that melt-in-your-mouth smoked chicken that had been marinated in pineapple juice and coated with her secret concoction of herbs and spices? Or something equally delectable? Apparently, Erika figured the most effective way to coax a man out of his property was to sabotage his taste buds and his stomach.

Judd focused on Erika's face. Her face was wholesome and animated and her eyes reminded him of a cloudless sky. Her ivory skin, dotted with freckles on her upturned nose, made her look fragile and delicate—a blatant contrast to her assertive, bubbly personality. She was part bombshell-in-hiding and part girl-next-door. A woman of interesting contrasts and potential.

Judd watched Erika balance the covered plate in one hand while she hammered on the front door with the other. He knew she wouldn't give up and go away, so he opened the door before she pounded a hole in it. "Now what?" he demanded.

Erika beamed an enthusiastic greeting as she sailed, uninvited, into his house.

The instant Judd felt himself leaning impulsively toward her, he withdrew and stiffened his resistance. "The answer is still no," he said right off.

Might as well beat her to the punch and hope she'd give up her ongoing crusade to buy his property. He didn't want her to sweet-talk him into signing over the old barn that held fond childhood memories. He didn't want to salivate like Pavlov's dogs when the aromatic smoked meat, piled beneath a layer of aluminum foil, whetted his appetite.

Undaunted, Erika thrust the heaping plate at him and smiled radiantly. "No, what? *No,* you won't do me a favor by taking this extra food off my hands? *No,* you've decided to stop eating altogether?"

She glanced around the gloomy living room, shook her head in disapproval, then strode to the west window. "Really, Judd, it should be a criminal offense to keep this grand old house enshrouded in darkness. It looks like vampire headquarters."

Leaving him holding the plate, she threw open the drapes, jerked up the blinds and opened all three living room windows. Fresh air poured into the room, carrying her scent to him. Judd winced when blinding sunbeams speared into the room, spotlighting Erika's alluring profile—as if he needed another reminder of how well proportioned she was.

He didn't. Furthermore, he didn't want to deal with the lusty thoughts her appearance provoked. He didn't want to like anything about Erika Dunn. Erika was too attractive, too optimistic. Too *everything* for a man who'd become cynical and world-weary after years of belly-crawling around hellholes in Third World countries.

He wondered what it was going to take to discourage Erika from waltzing in here as if she owned the place and trying to befriend a man who was completely unworthy of friendship. He hadn't been able to protect the one true friend he'd had in the past decade and that tormented him. He didn't want anyone to depend on him or expect anything from him.

He wasn't supposed to be there. It wasn't his night; in
fact, this week he wasn't supposed to deal with any emer-
gencies unless they occurred during normal office hours.

But because of a wedding, there'd been a shortage
of pediatricians to staff the pediatric emergency floor.
So, when his partner had asked, Quinton had agreed to
take Bart's shift. Even though it was a Friday night,
Quinton had nothing better to do.

Which, when he stopped to think about it, was pa-
thetic. He, Dr. Quinton Searle, pediatric specialist,
should have something to do. At thirty-five, he should
have some woman to date, some place to be, something.

But the truth was that he didn't, which was why,

when the call came through, he was in the wrong place at the right time. He turned to Elaine. He liked working with her. At fifty-something she'd seen it all, and was a model of brisk efficiency, the most reliable nurse in any crisis. "What have I got?" he asked.

"Four-year-old child. Poison Control just called. The kid ate the mother's cold medicine. Thought it was green candy."

He frowned as he contemplated the situation. "How many?"

Elaine checked her notes. "The mother thinks it was only two tablets, but she isn't sure. The container's empty."

Great, Quinton thought. He hated variables. "Is she here yet?"

Elaine shook her head. "Any minute. She's on her way. Downstairs knows to buzz me immediately so we can bring the kid right up."

Quinton nodded. "Downstairs" was slang for the main emergency room. As part of the Chicago Presbyterian Hospital's patient care plan, a separate emergency floor had been set up especially for children. Children were triaged in the main E.R., and then sent up to the pediatric E.R. He shoved his hand into the pocket of his white doctor's coat. "Let me know the minute you get the buzz."

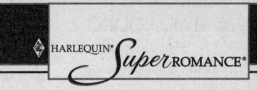

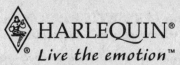

If you enjoyed what you just read,
then we've got an offer you can't resist!

Take 2 bestselling love stories FREE!
Plus get a FREE surprise gift!

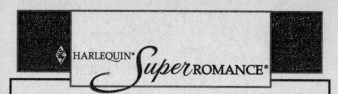

HARLEQUIN *Super*ROMANCE®

A new book by the critically acclaimed author of No Crystal Stair

Heart and Soul
by **Eva Rutland**
Harlequin Superromance #1255

Life is both wonderful and complicated when you're in love. Especially if you get involved with a business rival, as Jill Ferrell does. Scott Randall's a wealthy man and his background is very different from hers. But love can be even more difficult if, like Jill's friend Kris Gilroy, you fall for a man of a different race. She's black and Tom's white, and her family doesn't approve. But as both women learn, the heart makes its own choices....

Available in February 2005 wherever Harlequin books are sold.

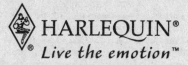

HARLEQUIN®
Live the emotion™

M Buie

HARLEQUIN *Super*ROMANCE®

A six-book series from Harlequin Superromance

WOMEN in Blue

Six female cops battling crime and corruption on the streets of Houston. Together they can fight the blue wall of silence. But divided, will they fall?

Coming in February 2005, *She Walks the Line* by Roz Denny Fox (Harlequin Superromance #1254)

As a Chinese woman in the Houston Police Department, Mei Lu Ling is a minority twice over. She once worked for her father, a renowned art dealer specializing in Asian artifacts, so her new assignment—tracking art stolen from Chinese museums—is a logical one. But when she's required to work with Cullen Archer, an insurance investigator connected to Interpol, her reaction is more emotional than logical. Because she could easily fall in love with this man…and his adorable twins.

Coming in March 2005, *A Mother's Vow* by K. N. Casper (Harlequin Superromance #1260)

There is corruption in Police Chief Catherine Tanner's department. So when evidence turns up to indicate that her husband may not have died of natural causes, she has to go outside her own precinct to investigate. Ex-cop Jeff Rowan is the most logical person for her to turn to. Unfortunately, Jeff isn't inclined to help Catherine, considering she was the one who fired him.

Available wherever Harlequin books are sold.

Also in the series:
The Partner by Kay David (#1230, October 2004)
The Children's Cop by Sherry Lewis (#1237, November 2004)
The Witness by Linda Style (#1243, December 2004)
Her Little Secret by Anna Adams (#1248, January 2005)